HARBOUR MY

Ar fell in love when she
sev
when she learned that the man she wanted thought of her as a foolish, romantic child. But she could not escape the constant reminders of her youthful folly, for her life was irrevocably intertwined with Guy Carlow's when he became her trustee and virtual guardian. Their attitude to each other was always poised precariously on the line between love and hate ... the thin line of indifference that needed so little encouragement for emotions to topple one way or another. Antonia did not mean to make the mistake of loving him again ... and she sought a safe harbour for her heart in marriage to another man ...

HARBOUR MY HEART

Paula Lindsay

CHIVERS LARGE PRINT
BATH

Library of Congress Cataloging-in-Publication Data

Lindsay, Paula.
  Harbour my heart / Paula Lindsay.
    p. (large print)   cm.
  ISBN 0–7927–1804–6.—ISBN 0–7927–1805–4 (hardcover)
  1. Man–woman relationships—Fiction.
  2. Large type books.
I. Title.
[PS3562.I511916H37   1993]
813'.54—dc20   93–28616
                                            CIP

British Library Cataloguing in Publication Data available

This Large Print edition is published by Chivers Press, England, and by
Curley Large Print, an imprint of Chivers North America, 1993.

Published by arrangement with the author.

U.K. Hardcover ISBN 0 7451 2041 5
U.K. Softcover   ISBN 0 7451 2053 9
U.S. Hardcover ISBN 0 7927 1805 4
U.S. Softcover   ISBN 0 7927 1804 6

Printed in Great Britain

HARBOUR MY HEART

CHAPTER ONE

Mersleigh End was a small and rather pretty village in very rural surroundings but it was little more than twenty miles from the heart of London ... an ideal situation for those who liked to live in the country but also liked to be within easy reach of the city.

Newcomers to the area were usually surprised by the narrow, winding lanes and the unexpectedly steep hills that confronted them once they left the main arterial road for the quieter route to the village and they were inclined to drive cautiously through the verdant countryside.

Antonia knew her way too well to slacken her speed or to take particular care and she drove at her usual headlong pace along the quiet lanes that were touched to beauty by the advent of spring. She passed only the occasional car and a few people on foot as she drove past the peaceful little cottages and quiet farms and long stretches of sunlit fields.

It was a warm and sunny afternoon with all the promise of the summer that was now not so distant and she had dropped the hood of her low-slung, scarlet sports car and shed the jacket of her neat, tailored suit.

1

Her mood did not match the day, however ... for her face was stormy and her eyes glittering with temper and the tautness of anger touched every line of her slender body. She scarcely heeded her surroundings for she was consumed with annoyance and impatience ... and it was not until she rounded the final bend and saw the old church of St. Stephen to her left that she realised that she had covered those twenty-two miles from town and was already in Mersleigh End.

Her destination lay just beyond the village ... a long, low, white-painted house standing well back from the road in its own grounds, framed by trees and well-kept lawns and well-stocked flower beds. It was the home of Sir Guy Carlow, author and playwright— and the most detestable man she knew, Antonia thought bitterly as she turned into the long, sweeping drive.

As she stepped from the car and slammed the door with quite unnecessary violence, Eva Standen rose from her knees beside the flower-bed that she had been weeding and glanced at her beautiful, wilful daughter with some trepidation. It was all very well for Guy to claim that she should be inured to Antonia's tantrums ... it was quite usual for him to remove himself from the vicinity before the storm broke and Eva was left to bear the brunt.

Antonia moved swiftly towards her mother. 'Where is he?' she demanded furiously.

Eva stifled a sigh and managed to smile a welcome.

'Isn't it a lovely day? But the weeds are running riot after all the rain ... I couldn't ignore them any longer. Guy? I believe he's in his study ... or he may have gone out. I really don't know, dear,' she added vaguely.

'Of course I mean Guy!' Antonia snapped impatiently. 'Do you know what he's done? Oh, I could *kill* him! I'm sick to death of his interference!'

Eva's heart sank for she could not bear the frequent, bitter quarrels. 'You know he means well, dear,' she said weakly. 'If only you would discuss things with him calmly, I'm sure ...' She broke off for Antonia had little patience with her mother's gentle, trusting nature when she was out of temper and she had turned away abruptly to walk towards the house.

Eva looked after her, anxiety touching her blue eyes. She was a small, frail woman with the soft and delicate colouring that was supposed to be representative of English womanhood. In her youth, she had been a remarkably pretty girl and she was still a very pretty woman. She was a quiet and sensitive person with an instinctive readiness to find excuses for the faults or mistakes of others

3

... and she knew that nothing aggravated her daughter more than the affection and gratitude and loyalty that she felt towards Guy Carlow. She wondered now what had happened to cause that blaze of anger in Antonia's beautiful eyes ... and comforted herself with the thought that Guy could cope admirably with her in such moods when he did not choose to add fuel to the fire by walking away with a sardonic smile and a careless comment to the effect that he would be very well pleased to talk to her when she had regained her temper...

Antonia went directly to the study and threw open the door, scarcely expecting to find Guy at his desk and busy with a sheaf of galley-proofs.

He glanced up with a faint frown in his dark eyes. Recognising her mood, he laid down his pen and amusement flickered briefly about his mouth. 'Well? What is it now?' he asked carelessly.

'I want to talk to you!' she flared, taut with anger.

He glanced at his watch ... a gesture that fanned her fury to white heat as he had known it would. 'I can spare ten minutes.'

'That will suffice,' she said crisply. 'It doesn't take long to tell you exactly what I think of your abominable, high-handed, insufferable interference in my affairs!'

'I'm pleased to hear it ... I'm very busy

just now,' he said mildly. 'Vent your spleen, my dear … I can see it is choking you.'

She threw him a venomous glance. 'How dare you cancel my order for a new Sabre?' she demanded passionately. 'How dare you humiliate me so? What do you mean by informing Sutton that I won't be requiring the new car when you know very well that I've talked of nothing else for days!'

'So much temper for a mere trifle?' he asked mockingly.

'A trifle? Can you imagine how I felt when Sutton told me … how foolish I appeared?'

'You will appear much more foolish if you reach the age of twenty-five to find yourself without a penny to your name,' he told her drily. His eyes narrowed abruptly as she glanced at him with impatient contempt. 'What the devil do you mean by placing an order for a new car without consulting me?' he asked quietly but with the hint of anger behind the words.

Antonia coloured slightly. 'Without asking your permission, do you mean?' she taunted fiercely.

He smiled faintly, mockingly. 'Exactly.'

Seething, she threw herself into an armchair and stripped off her gloves. 'Intolerable!' she stormed. 'I hate this stupid, impossible, humiliating trust business.'

'No more than I do, Antonia,' he said wryly. 'Or do you suppose that I enjoy doling

5

out your allowance each quarter and having to quarrel with you each time you embark on an extravagance that you simply cannot afford.'

'You are ridiculous!' she returned coldly. 'My father left me a great deal of money...'

'Which you are endeavouring to get through in the shortest possible time,' he broke in impatiently. 'As your trustee, I am responsible for ensuring that you still have a great deal of money when you are twenty-five. I should be failing your father's trust in me to allow you to spend it all before that date. Have you any idea how much you have managed to get through, with my permission, since his death? You are madly extravagant ... and you simply do not need a new Sabre when last year's model is in excellent condition.'

'Last year's model!' she said with disgust. 'A pretty figure I shall cut when all my friends are driving about in their new cars!'

'All your friends ...' he said slowly. 'That is just the trouble, Antonia. You must always outshine everyone ... the newest, the best, the most expensive. I have been very patient, very indulgent with your whims ... but you simply don't know where to draw the line. So I must draw it for you...'

White-faced, her eyes blazing, she turned on him. 'How contemptible you are! Patient, indulgent ... how *dare* you! The money is

6

mine and I have the right to spend it as I choose! My father merely intended that you should be my banker ... not that you should be able to tell me how and when I may spend the money he left me!'

'You are mistaken,' he said coolly. 'Your father knew you very well ... and the terms of his will were explicit. I am not merely your banker, my dear ... I have the right to dispense or withhold the money as I choose until you are twenty-five.' Suddenly he smiled ... and his was a very warm and attractive smile that redeemed the rather harsh and forbidding features. 'Why must you fight it, Antonia ... you cannot change matters and I would not if I could, you know.'

'Holding the whip-hand over me is very much to your liking!' she flared.

His smile faded. 'You know that I deplored this business as much as you at first ... but I soon realised that it was a very sensible arrangement. You are reckless and impulsive and much too generous to your friends. Someone has to keep your spending in check ... someone has to keep a firm hand on your rein—and Eva is certainly not suited to the task. She could never deny you anything ... but I can and will.' He picked up his pen and began to glance over the proofs once more, bored with an argument that was all too familiar ... and Antonia

7

glared at him with angry hatred.

'So I am not to have the new car?'

'Not unless you can find the money to pay for it,' he said drily.

She rose abruptly. 'I shall find it,' she said tautly.

He looked at her mockingly. 'Now what devilry have you in mind?'

Her chin tilted. 'I'm sick of coming to you, cap in hand, whenever I want anything ... and there's one way I can put an end to this humiliating business. Fortunately, I don't need your consent to my marriage ... and I know plenty of men who will be delighted to marry me!'

Guy raised a quizzical eyebrow. 'Do you indeed? Well, I wish you very happy, my dear ... and I shall be thankful to bestow you and all your extravagances on the poor devil that you choose to marry. I only hope he can afford you ... for you do understand that not even marriage before you reach twenty-five has the power to break my control over your money?'

'I've checked that point with Edmundson,' she retorted crisply. 'The man I have in mind can afford to ignore my lack of money.'

He smiled faintly. 'Leo Bryce, I gather.'

'You're so perceptive,' she taunted.

'You're very transparent,' he returned drily. 'Does Eva know of your plans?'

'Of course not! Do you doubt that she

8

would have hurried to tell you the news? What a relief it will be to you both to be rid of me!'

His eyes darkened with anger. But he merely said carelessly: 'Very true ... but I expect you will be back with us very shortly. Bryce is not noted for his constancy, after all.'

'You've never cared for Leo—either of you,' she said impatiently.

'I'm surprised that you do! But you have never been selective in your friends ... and I suppose it was inevitable that you should choose to marry a rake with an unsavoury reputation and three previous marriages to his credit.'

She smiled sweetly. 'But of course! I should be bored to tears by a man of integrity and good character ... which is exactly what you and Eva have always had in mind for me, isn't it?'

'Heaven forbid that you should be bored,' he said caustically.

'Exactly my own sentiments!' she returned mockingly. She moved towards the door, slender and graceful in the neat, short skirt and cool lemon blouse, youthful and vibrantly beautiful with her copper-coloured hair curling lightly on her shoulders and her creamy skin and the stormy eyes that could change from grey to green with her moods. 'I've over-run my ten minutes and dare not

9

take up any more of your valuable time,' she added lightly.

She closed the door on the words and went to her room, still seething but also slightly alarmed by the wild and angry impulse that had urged her to declare that she meant to marry Leo Bryce...

Leo was amusing and exciting and the danger of encouraging his attentions added a certain spice to life. She knew that he wanted her desperately—but she doubted if any thought of marrying her had ever crossed his mind and she hoped she was not so foolish as to contemplate becoming the fourth wife of a man with so little respect for women. Guy had reacted to her announcement with irritating indifference but she knew he would gladly bring her affair with Leo to an end if he could. He had recognised her words as an attempt at blackmail and he did not believe that she would marry Leo ... but if she could contrive to coax Leo into a convenient engagement it would be an exquisite amusement to observe Guy's attempts to prevent the marriage. For he would consider it his duty to her father to do all he could to stop her taking such a disastrous step ... and she had been amply provided with evidence that he took his duties as her trustee and virtual guardian very seriously.

He was so utterly hateful ... she did not know what she had ever done to deserve such treatment at her father's hands! How could he have given Guy so much power over her actions and her affairs? How could he have been so insensitive to her feelings, her humiliation and helpless fury, her hatred of the man he had regarded as the next best thing to a son?

She had never liked Guy Carlow ... except when she was very young and foolish enough to suppose herself in love with him. She had soon realised her mistake when he made it painfully obvious that he considered her little more than a foolish, romantic child. She could still writhe at the memory of the mocking lift of his eyebrow, the faint smile that quirked the hard yet sensual mouth, the amused indulgence in his dark eyes when she was so insane as to blurt out the way she felt about him ... at seventeen, one's emotions were very intense and of course she had known that he was much too old for her, that there were plenty of younger men who could fulfil her youthful dreams of romance, that there were several years before she needed to bother her head with thoughts of marriage—but the love he had inspired had turned to sudden and blinding hatred when he had told her as much, gently and kindly but with undeniable and amused patronage.

He was cold and ruthless and arrogant, lacking in sensitivity or understanding, impatient and demanding and autocratic ...

and she would never understand why her father had valued his friendship so much and regarded him with so much affection and trust—or why her mother should imbue him with so many good qualities and be so fond of him and so content to share the same roof with him.

It had been Guy's suggestion that they should sell the Little Manor at Wittingdean, some ten miles away, and share his home at Mersleigh End. Her mother was too used to having all her decisions made for her to object ... and Antonia, dependent on him for every penny and too proud at that time to ask his permission to take a flat in town, had not been consulted. Later, she had made the suggestion of a flat of her own ... and he had refused, reminding her that her father had intended him to look after her until she was twenty-five and he could scarcely carry out that duty if she was footloose in London with a host of disreputable friends to lead her astray. She had flouted that refusal by making a point of staying with various friends for weeks at a time ... but she had found it an expensive business, for the friends he despised did not lack for money and did not hesitate to spend it extravagantly, and it was a matter of pride with Antonia to compete with their spending.

She had quarrelled frequently with Guy

over his refusals to supplement her generous allowance—and eventually, knowing that he could withdraw that allowance entirely if he chose to do so, she had given in with a bad grace. She lived with Guy and her mother at Mersleigh End ... but spent much of her time in the company of her friends.

It was a difficult situation for a girl of twenty-two who was both proud and self-willed ... and she was too used to considering her own interests to realise that it was also very difficult for Guy Carlow. She was convinced that he disliked and disapproved of her and did all he could to make things awkward for her. And it was awkward to know that few of her friends were welcome at her home, that she did not even have an ally in her mother who was always so swift to defend, to excuse, to blind herself to any fault in Guy ... and to be always conscious that anything she might want that could not be met by her allowance must receive Guy's approval and consent.

To be fair, he frequently paid her bills without comment and even increased her allowance from time to time without request ... and she never really knew if the money he provided came always from the funds he held in trust for her or occasionally from his own income for he was a wealthy man, partly by inheritance, partly by his own efforts.

But there had also been many quarrels

when he refused to agree that she could need or must have some particular extravagance ... and it never ceased to bewilder Antonia that her loving and indulgent father could have been so blinded by his affection for Guy Carlow, or so insensitive to the humiliation he had inflicted on his daughter, by instigating that ridiculous trust which was nevertheless perfectly legal and must be endured for another three years!

CHAPTER TWO

Once more, Guy laid down his pen. He rose and strolled to the open window that overlooked the lawns and flower-beds that were always kept in such excellent order.

Eva was weeding ... her small, slight figure bent industriously over the rich earth. His eyes softened as he studied her ... dear Eva, so gentle, so placid, so kind-hearted and sensitive and so anxious that everything should always run smoothly. It always amazed him that she should have produced a daughter like the tempestuous and temperamental Antonia who swept through life, taking all that came her way as her natural due, wilful and selfish and arrogant ... and much too beautiful for her own good, he thought wryly. She was cast very much in the mould of her father, of course—but Philip Standen had possessed many redeeming qualities. He had been quick tempered ... but swift to repent, to apologise, to atone. Antonia would never admit that she might be at fault ... and he did not believe that she could ever be brought to acknowledge or apologise for any lapse. Philip had made money and spent it with ease ... but he had been cautious enough to set aside a substantial sum for his wife and daughter. Antonia had inherited his impulsive generosity but not his instinctive dislike and unerring recognition of those who sought to take advantage of that generosity. Philip had possessed the natural arrogance of birth and breeding but he had never allowed it to affect his dealings with people who were less fortunate than himself ... Antonia was inclined to despise such people. Certainly her friends were all people with money and good social status ... and it was no novelty for Antonia's name or likeness to appear in the society magazines, linked with one or other of a set who seemed to devote their entire time to enjoyment and the spending of money and the expected social roundabout. Philip had been secure in a position which enabled him to say or do much as he pleased without fear of criticism or censure ... but he had been a kindly and sensitive man who hesitated to wound anyone by word or deed, a man who would go out of his way to help anyone, friend or stranger, a man who had been much loved, much admired and always respected by all who knew him.

Many had mourned the death of the famous actor who had made his name in silent films and progressed to become one of the brightest stars of stage and screen. Guy had mourned the loss to the theatrical world ... but he had grieved sincerely for the loss of his friend. They had worked together originally on the adaptation of one of Guy's novels for the theatre ... and he had taken Philip Standen's advice and turned to writing plays as well as the successful historical novels for which he was famous. They had become close friends despite the considerable age gap ... and it had been little surprise to Guy to learn that Philip had appointed him as trustee and virtual guardian to his daughter in his will. But he had accepted the responsibility with a great deal of reluctance ... for he knew, if Antonia did not, that it had been Philip's constant hope that his daughter might marry the man who had become as dear as a son to him.

Had Philip really supposed that constant contact with each other would achieve the desired result? He must have known that Antonia would never marry a man she had never forgiven for mishandling her youthful claim to love him, he thought drily ... but

16

perhaps Philip had been misled by his daughter's swift and baffling changes of mood that enabled her to play the coquette with a man she detested and with whom she might have crossed swords only moments before. It had happened so often ... one moment, she was blazing with fury and hurling insults at his head—the next, she was laughing and crying pax and holding out her hands in swift appeal for his response to her change of mood. She was a baffling, bewitching, aggravating little minx ... for all her many faults, it was impossible for him not to love her ... except when he was itching to wring that slender, lovely neck!

He had always loved her ... even when she was little more than a child. He had always known that she was the only woman in the world he could love and wish to keep by his side for the rest of his life. But it had been impossible for him to take advantage of the impetuous, youthful, headlong plunge into first love ... he had hoped she might come to love him in truth when she was older, more experienced, more mature but he had not bargained for that impulsive infatuation and he had been at a loss to know how to cope with it successfully. The sudden reversal of her emotions had not been unexpected ... but he had believed that time would heal her wound and bring her to regard him with less hatred and contempt. He had been wrong, he thought ruefully ... and he had long since resigned himself to loving the girl he could never hope to marry.

He knew she had no intention of marrying Leo Bryce ... and he doubted if the man even meant to suggest marriage. Antonia had merely thrown that taunt at his head in anger, the impulse of the moment, presumably an attempt at blackmail for she must know that he would do almost anything to prevent such a marriage ... except rescind his decision about the car, he thought grimly.

Antonia was neither so stupid nor so reckless as to link her life with a man like Bryce, he assured himself confidently. She would not make that kind of mistake ... and he hoped that she was making no mistakes of any kind where Bryce was concerned. She had been frequently in the man's company in recent weeks and no doubt she was attracted by his good looks and undeniable charm and forceful appeal for women and flattered by the interest of a man with many affairs to his credit. But he did not believe that Antonia was the man's mistress ... although he had no way of knowing how generous she might be to the men in her life. He knew she was impulsive and headstrong and determined to lead her life without interference but he would be very reluctant to believe that she was reckless with her favours. Flirtation came as naturally to her as breathing, of course ... but he rather felt that she was one of those women who promised much and gave little. The danger lay in her falling in love with Bryce ... for she was young enough to believe that love covered a multitude of sins and was sufficient excuse for ignoring the principles of her upbringing.

He could only hope that she would keep both her heart and her head. He had no control over her emotions and no right to object to anything she chose to do where her personal life was concerned ... but he did object very forcibly to the thought of her falling prey to Bryce's unmistakable intent. She was spoiled and selfish and damnably difficult to handle ... but he had no wish to see her hurt by such a man or to know that she was capable of plunging into a disastrous affair with a notorious rake ...

He stepped on to the terrace as the little maid that Eva had recently acquired appeared with the tea-tray. She was very young and very shy but Eva was pleased with her willingness to learn ... and Guy could overlook the girl's strange apprehension of him and the occasional crash of china in the distance. He smiled at her encouragingly ... and hastened to take the tray from her suddenly nerveless hands. He did not know why she stood in so much awe of him and he was faintly amused although he regretted her nervous embarrassment in his presence.

19

'All right, Sally, I'll take it.'

'Thank you, sir.' She relinquished the tray with an anguished glance over its setting ... and hurried away as though she expected him to find fault with it.

He set down the tray, glancing at his watch. 'Eva ...!' he called and she turned her head to smile and nod. Within a few moments, she rose to her feet, pulling off her gardening gloves, and walked across the lawn to join him on the terrace, slender as a girl in the silk dress she wore, brushing a strand of her fine, blonde hair from her eyes with a naturally graceful gesture.

She sat down and accepted tea with a smile. 'Thank you, Guy ... just what I need. How nice this is,' she said appreciatively, lifting her face to the warm sunshine. 'It seems such a long time since we drank our tea on the terrace.'

'It has been a long winter,' he agreed lightly, smiling at her.

'The garden is looking quite pretty, don't you think? This warm spell after the rain is bringing everything out. I'm very pleased with the success I've had with the bedding plants. You don't think it's a little early to put them out, do you, Guy?' she added anxiously. 'We might yet have some frost in the early mornings, I suppose.'

'I expect they'll survive. But I wouldn't presume to advise you, my dear Eva ... you

20

know so much more than I do about such things,' he said, producing his cigarettes and offering the case. 'What does Barlow think?'

She took a cigarette and bent her head over the flame of his lighter. 'Oh, he agrees that they seem quite hardy ... but you know he always agrees with me, Guy. I don't think he has the heart to object to anything I suggest.' She laughed softly. 'He's such a dear old man ... I can wind him round my little finger, I'm afraid.'

'Without even trying,' Guy said, his eyes twinkling. 'Whereas he always regards me with utter contempt and before you came here considered the garden to be particularly his own province!'

'Oh, I'm sure that isn't true,' she said swiftly, reproachfully. 'That he regards you with contempt, I mean ... no one *could*, Guy!'

He laughed. 'You are forgetting Antonia,' he said ruefully. He had known that she was avoiding any mention of her daughter ... she shrank from any unpleasantness and seemed to consider that she must be entirely to blame for the wilful streak in Antonia that made it impossible for her to be with Guy for any length of time without provoking a quarrel.

She looked at him swiftly. 'Have you seen her today?'

He nodded. 'She bearded me in my den,'

21

he said carelessly.

'I'm afraid she was a little upset,' Eva said tentatively.

He smiled at the understatement. 'My back is very broad, you know,' he said reassuringly. 'Did she tell you why she was ... a little upset?'

'No ... she seemed very anxious to see you,' she said ruefully.

Guy looked at her with sympathy in his dark eyes. He knew and deplored Antonia's lack of patience where Eva was concerned ... and he also knew that the mother assumed full responsibility for all of the lovely daughter's faults. In fact, many of those faults were inherited from Philip—and they had never been checked or corrected when Antonia was a child because she had been born to affectionate and indulgent parents who had been incapable of denying her anything, partly because they adored her and partly because she had discovered at an early age that a tantrum at an inconvenient moment could bring swift fulfilment of her desires. Fortunately, Antonia had a warm and generous heart and an attractive personality to combat the effect of such spoiling so she had not turned out as impossible as she might have done ... and Guy was convinced that most of her faults could be eradicated with the right handling.

'I cancelled the new car,' he said quietly. 'I

didn't think the expenditure was justified ...
but I didn't expect Antonia to see my point
of view, of course.'

'Without telling her? Oh, Guy ... was that
kind?' she asked gently, anxious that he
should not suppose her to be criticising him
and yet very sensitive to her daughter's
reaction to such high-handed treatment.

'Perhaps not ... but she really shouldn't
order these things without consulting me,
you know,' he said with equal gentleness.

'No, of course not ... that was very
wrong,' she agreed. 'But she is so impulsive
... I'm sure she didn't mean to offend you,
Guy. I don't suppose she thought you would
object.'

His mouth quirked with amusement. 'She
intended to annoy me, Eva dear ... it was
retaliation for our last difference of opinion
when I routed her without compunction.
She knew I would object ... but she didn't
expect me to cancel her order.'

'You've never done so before,' she
reminded him quietly.

'No ... more's the pity,' he said, a little
grimly. 'Perhaps she will hesitate in future
when she feels the impulse to order
something quite unnecessary and grossly
expensive.'

She was silent for a moment. Then she
said hesitantly: 'Her friends are so
extravagant and naturally she likes to keep

23

pace with them ... she is very young, Guy.'

He was touched by the hint of pleading in her soft voice. But he knew it would be fatal to allow his resolution to be swayed... having made the stand, he must adhere to it. It was not merely a matter of a new car at stake ... it was time that Antonia ceased to regard him as little more than an indulgent money machine with unlimited funds at her disposal, he thought with faint bitterness.

'Her allowance enables her to keep pace with her friends in most things,' he said quietly, reasonably. 'But I fail to see why she needs to change her car every six months or so simply because her friends do so.'

But Eva's thoughts had followed a new direction and now she said abruptly: 'I wish she hadn't met that awful man in Monte Carlo, Guy ... I can't like that friendship, you know.'

He shrugged. 'She would have met him—or someone equally as dis-reputable—as easily in London, Eva.'

'How can she encourage him ... when all the world knows what he is!' she said indignantly.

'That kind of man is obviously attractive to women ... and like most women, Antonia prides herself on being able to handle him with consummate skill,' he said drily.

'Do you suppose ... ?' Eva began tentatively—and broke off, catching her underlip between her pretty teeth.

'That the affair is serious?' he finished lightly. He smiled warmly, reassuringly. 'No, I don't.'

'I suppose he is attractive,' she said doubtfully.

'Most women would appear to think so,' he agreed carelessly. 'Antonia says that she is going to marry him, by the way.'

Eva stared at him, dismay touching her eyes. 'Does she?'

'She threw it at my head,' he said, smiling. 'I think she was taken aback when I wished her happy and sent my condolences to Bryce.'

'Oh, Guy!' she exclaimed reproachfully ... but a little gurgle of laughter escaped her as she thought of Antonia's undoubted reaction to such tactics. Then she said anxiously: 'Can he really want to marry her, Guy?'

'I doubt if he can afford another wife,' he said indifferently.

'But Antonia will be a wealthy woman when she is twenty-five!'

'That isn't for three years—and Bryce has never managed to maintain his interest in any woman for more than six months. I don't imagine that her money appeals to him, Eva ... or the thought of paying maintenance to a fourth ex-wife! You've no need to be anxious ... Antonia won't marry him.'

'There are worse things,' she said, almost beneath her breath.

He stubbed his cigarette. 'Oh, Antonia can take care of herself,' he said carelessly ... and hoped that his confidence was not misplaced.

Eva glanced towards the house. 'I wonder if Sally told Antonia that we were having tea on the terrace this afternoon.'

'Probably. If she means to join us she will do so ... when she has sufficiently controlled her temper,' he returned indifferently.

Even as he spoke, Antonia came out to the terrace. She walked towards them, smiling, self-possessed, light-hearted confidence in every step, her beautiful hair dancing on her shoulders as she moved with lithe and youthful grace.

Eva smiled a welcome, affection and admiration in her eyes, and obvious relief touching her expression as she realised that the storm was over for the moment.

It never failed to surprise her that Guy and Antonia could meet after an angry exchange without the least acrimony in their manner to each other ... and she supposed she would never really understand Antonia's moods or cease to marvel at Guy's patience and tolerance and competent handling of a very difficult situation...

CHAPTER THREE

Antonia was swift to repent but much too proud to acknowledge a fault or to apologise for anything she might say or do in temper.

She realised she should not have ordered a new car without discussing it with Guy ... but that was the result of a quarrel over something so trivial she could not now remember its cause. But she had been very angry with him and very resentful of the right her father had invested in Guy Carlow to take her to task over her friendships, her amusements, her way of life, her expenditure and her careless disregard for anyone's comfort or concerns but her own. She had ordered the new model of the Sabre on an impulse ... partly because a friend was already driving one and partly because she wanted to declare an independence of Guy that she simply could not possess in such intolerable circumstances.

It had never occurred to her that he would quietly cancel the order ... he had never done such a thing before ... and she had talked airily and confidently of her impatience to acquire the new car without incurring any comment other than the mocking lift of an eyebrow and a faintly sardonic smile.

She had called at the sales rooms in Piccadilly to hasten delivery ... and she had been stunned and humiliated and plunged into the heat of anger by the information that Sir Guy Carlow had cancelled the car on her behalf three days before. She scarcely knew how she had kept her temper but apart from advising Sutton of the dangers of accepting cancellations without first checking with the buyer, she had said very little ... for all that needed to be said must be saved for Guy's ears.

But she had wasted her breath, of course ... her abuse left him unmoved if not amused and she was powerless to force him to pay for a new car if he chose not to do so. How on earth had she managed to annoy him so intensely that he sought to punish her with such vindictive measures! They had certainly quarrelled ... and she supposed she might have said some pretty scathing things in the heat of the moment. But they had quarrelled so many times—when he could be persuaded to draw swords instead of walking away with an infuriating taunt that left her speechless with anger. One could not force a quarrel on Guy ... and that was only one of the things about him that she detested. There was nothing more frustrating than to be filled with anger and to be denied its rightful target!

She wondered if it could be true that she

was spending at such an alarming rate that she might be penniless by the time she was twenty-five. Rapidly she ran over in her mind some of the wilder extravagances of the past year ... the car which she had allowed a mere acquaintance to borrow and which he had crashed, killing himself and wrecking the car beyond repair: that impulsive flight to New York in pursuit of a man who had attracted her forcibly only to find that he was married and not at all pleased to see her: the money she had lost at the Casino in Monte Carlo: the beautiful and expensive mare that she had forced over a high fence with the result that she had been thrown and badly concussed and the mare had broken her back and had to be shot ... Antonia sighed as conscience twinged unexpectedly. It was a shock to realise how much those things amounted to ... and there were so many she simply couldn't remember.

It was scarcely surprising that Guy declared himself to have been both patient and indulgent, she thought drily. It was much more cause for astonishment that he had not taken her to task long before!

She supposed she had been rather reckless of late. She really must make some effort to cut down her expenses ... but she had to have clothes and jewels and furs and one could not accept the invitations of her friends without giving in return and there were always so many other demands on her purse. Her allowance was considerable but it was astonishing how rapidly it dwindled.

But she simply must have the new Sabre. Guy did not understand how humiliating it would be to drive an old model when all her friends were acquiring new ones! One simply could not force Guy into things but perhaps he could be persuaded...?

With rising confidence, she went to join Guy and her mother on the terrace. Guy rose with his instinctive courtesy ... their eyes met and held for a long moment and then she laughed up at him, her lovely eyes dancing with merriment. 'Brute!' she accused lightly. 'You ruined my afternoon, you know!'

'I'm sorry for it,' he said quietly. 'But we could have avoided this contretemps, Antonia.'

She sat down and regarded him with faintly mocking eyes. 'If I had chosen to tell you that I wanted to change my car?'

'Exactly.' He resumed his own seat. 'I should have dissuaded you, of course ... but we need not have quarrelled over it.'

Antonia chuckled. 'You may believe that—I don't!' She leaned forward to place a hand on his arm, smiling at him with eyes that were suddenly warm and coaxing. 'Oh, Guy don't be mean,' she said pleadingly. 'I've told everyone that I'm getting the car

30

... just think how embarrassing it will be for me to admit that you won't allow me to have it.'

He was unmoved by the warmth in her lovely eyes, by the touch of her slim hand, by the pleading in her voice. 'Then don't admit it,' he said lightly. 'Merely claim to have changed your mind ... it's a woman's prerogative, after all.'

Her eyes flashed but she stifled the retort that trembled on her lips ... and Guy looked at her coolly, the sardonic smile mocking the strategy which would not succeed where temper had failed ...

Antonia dropped her hand and looked away, piqued by his indifference to the looks and the charm that had never failed to win her what she wanted except where he was concerned. He did not seem to admire the loveliness that captivated other men ... and when she could not fall back on the charm that was usually so successful she felt a little at a loss.

She shook her head to the offer of tea with slight impatience and sat silent as Guy turned to talk to her mother. She studied him, angry and resentful and a little annoyed by the unfailing courtesy and quiet affection and gentle consideration that he showed to her mother.

He thought her difficult and temperamental, self-willed and uncooperative,

31

Antonia thought crossly ... it did not seem to occur to him that he could also be difficult and uncooperative. He was certainly not an easy man to know or to like ... he was too cold, too reserved, too austere in his approach to life and to people. He did not give friendship or affection or trust very easily—no one could call him an impulsive man—but once given they were not withdrawn without excellent reason.

It seemed that they were destined to be antagonists rather than friends, Antonia decided, rather wryly ... she could never be sure that he liked her at all or that his interest and concern were any more than dutiful and it was much more likely that she was merely the constant thorn in his side that he frequently implied. She knew she had no appeal for him as a woman. She supposed he was basically indifferent to her, taking her very much for granted as a necessary inconvenience in his life ... and this was only to be expected from a man who had known her since she was little more than a child. But it provoked her for she could combat animosity and cope with admiration but indifference baffled and infuriated her.

There were many occasions when she wished he were not so immune to her attractions nor so impervious to her mischievous attempts to flirt with him as she did with other men. For she had learnt at an early age that her looks and her charm and her instinctive coquetry were valuable assets in acquiring whatever she wanted. It was not that he disliked women ... he had enjoyed several affairs but successfully avoided any serious entanglement.

Antonia would not resent his attitude to her so much if she was not compelled to witness his courteous and considerate attentions to other women—and compare them with his careless, cool and very casual approach to herself. She had yet to observe any glow of admiration for her in his dark eyes and anything in his manner that could be construed as interest or affection ... and although it could not hurt it could and did annoy!

He was an attractive man when he chose to smile, to unbend, to allow warmth and animation to touch his rather harsh features ... and even Antonia, much as she disliked him and scorned to admit that he could still attract her now that she was no longer seventeen, could not be entirely immune to his physical magnetism. As the writer of best-selling novels and long-running plays, it was inevitable that he should be very much in demand. But Antonia admitted that if he had lacked celebrity status he would still have been a very popular and well-liked man for he did not lack for charm and he seemed to draw people to him like a magnet, inspiring liking and admiration and affection without any seeming effort on his part.

Sometimes she discovered that she was warming to him, regretting their lack of sympathy and understanding ... but she had only to remind herself of the many times he had thwarted her, criticised her, humiliated and infuriated her for her to realise that she could never really regard him as anything but difficult and detestable ...

Eva glanced apprehensively at her daughter's stormy expression and wondered once more how she and Philip had managed to produce such a tempestuous personality. One never really knew what Antonia would say or do next ... and Eva seemed to live in constant dread that her daughter would create the kind of scandal that would ruin her chances of the good marriage that she hoped for Antonia. Could she really be thinking of marrying Leo Bryce? Guy did not seem to be anxious ... and one could always rely on his judgment. But Antonia was so impulsive, so careless of public opinion. Neither she nor Guy had made the mistake of actively opposing her friendship with the man but their disapproval had been obvious ... and nothing was more likely to goad Antonia into reckless behaviour than disapproval. But it was asking too much to expect them to approve of a man with his reputation!

There were plenty of young men with the right background and financial stability to make them acceptable to any mother ... but Antonia claimed to be bored by 'nice young men' and she always seemed to be attracted to the type of man that Eva instinctively mistrusted. Playing with fire was all very well and Antonia seemed to have escaped burning her fingers so far ... but Leo Bryce was a particularly dangerous flame with his good looks, his easy and practised charm and his careless disregard for anything but his own desires. With such similar attitudes and outlooks, Antonia must have been an easy conquest ... and she was obviously infatuated. But Eva thought unhappily that she would rather be told that Antonia was his mistress than that she was planning to marry such a man ... which was a very marked indication of her dislike and distrust of Leo Bryce.

If only she would fall in love with some wholly acceptable young man and settle down happily ... but Eva did not really suppose that her hope would be fulfilled so satisfactorily. Since adolescence Antonia had never failed to arouse anxiety and apprehension in her mother's mind and heart...

It was Eva Standen's dearest wish, never uttered and seldom admitted even to herself, that Antonia would fall in love with Guy.

She did not imagine that he loved Antonia but she felt that it would be impossible for him to resist doing so if only her lovely daughter would cease to antagonise and do battle with him and set herself to winning his affections. Men seemed to fall in love with Antonia with obliging promptness ... and Guy was a man like any other, after all.

She knew that Philip had always hoped for the match ... but he had been strangely maladroit in his unmistakable attempt to bring them together. She supposed one must be grateful that he had not made the fatal mistake of stipulating that Antonia must marry Guy in order to inherit her money ... for they were both proud and obstinate people and nothing on earth would have induced either of them to accede to such a stipulation.

Any mother could give her daughter to Guy Carlow with a thankful heart, she thought ... for he was so kind and considerate and understanding, so dependable, possessing so much strength of character and so much warmth of heart. Antonia was not old enough to know or appreciate the value of a man like Guy, she thought with faint impatience ... she was too easily swayed by a handsome face, by charm of manner, by extravagant and empty compliments, by the attentions of men she would be well advised to discourage.

Guy had so much more than looks and charm to recommend him, although Eva admitted that he had more than his fair share of the latter ... a woman could be not only happy but wholly secure as his wife—and one day Antonia might realise that the love and protection and tenderness she could find with Guy were much more to be valued than the ephemeral and doubtful admiration that men like Leo Bryce offered...

Her thoughts were given another direction as a car turned into the drive. Antonia sat up swiftly, brightening. But as it drew up behind her own, still parked in the drive, she relaxed and threw her mother a faintly mocking glance.

'It's the Ancient Mariner,' she said lightly. 'Calling on you, of course ... he is becoming particular in his attentions, isn't he? I really think you should ask him if his intentions are honourable, Guy!'

Guy quelled her with a glance while Eva, soft colour dawning in her cheeks, instinctively lifted her hands to her hair, too pleased and confused to pay any attention to her daughter's faintly sneering words. 'Am I tidy?' she asked anxiously.

Guy smiled at her gently. 'Are you ever anything else?' he teased.

'Gardening, you know ... makes one feel so grubby,' she explained ruefully ... and, smiling a warm welcome, rose and went to greet the elderly Commander Winch. He was a retired naval man with the weatherbeaten face of a man who had lived most of his life on the deck of a ship. He had only recently come to Mersleigh End to live with his brother, the vicar of St. Stephen's. Meeting Eva Standen and encountering her warm, shy smile, he had realised for the first time in his life what he had missed by never marrying. It was late in life to begin courting a woman and he had only his instinct to guide him, but he had found far more encouragement than he had dared to hope, for Eva had rapidly grown very fond of the kindly and courteous Commander.

'How nice to see you,' she said sincerely, holding out her hand.

He held her hand briefly, pleasure evident in his very blue eyes ... and then he turned abruptly and dived into the back of the car to re-appear with an armful of newly-dug rose trees.

'Brought you the roses I promised, my dear,' he said, a trifle brusquely. 'Hope I haven't called at an inconvenient moment?'

'Of course not ... how very kind,' Eva said warmly, touched by the speed with which he had carried out his promise. 'You must advise me on the best situation for them, Commander.' She was a little reluctant to accept the gift which he was holding out to her for he had not paused to remove the rich, damp earth from their roots.

Abruptly he realised ... as she conquered her instinctive fear of dirtying her dress and held out her arms to take the roses. 'No, no,' he said hastily.

'Your dress ... very thoughtless of me, Mrs. Standen. But you know that everything transplants successfully if one doesn't disturb the immediate earth about the roots. Perhaps I could lay them down somewhere for the time being.'

'Come and have some tea,' she suggested, linking her hand lightly in his arm.

'If I am not intruding...?'

She looked up at him reproachfully, fondly. 'What nonsense!' she exclaimed lightly. 'You know I am always glad to see you, Commander.'

'Nice of you to say so,' he said, a little gruffly. 'You have a kind heart, my dear.'

She laughed softly, coquettishly. 'It isn't mere kindness, you know ... you're a very eligible bachelor and every unattached woman in the neighbourhood is setting her cap for you!'

He chuckled, shaking his head. He was much too modest to take her words seriously but if he had had eyes for anyone but Eva Standen during the last few months he might have realised that every elderly spinster in the parish had experienced a fluttering heart on his arrival in Mersleigh End and regretted his obvious interest in the attractive widow...

CHAPTER FOUR

Guy rose to his feet, stretching out his hand, as Eva brought the Commander on to the terrace. He knew both liking and respect for the older man and the Commander's interest in Eva had his entire approval. He did not think it at all odd that she might wish to marry again ... and thought she could not do better than to marry a man who so obviously would do all in his power to make her happy.

'Good afternoon, Commander ... I can see that we shall soon have the best-stocked garden in the village,' he said lightly. 'Eva is very fond of roses, I know ... but you will never win the annual garden competition if you continue to supply us with your prize flowers.'

'Nonsense ... pleasure, I assure you,' the Commander returned briskly. 'Mrs. Standen shares my enthusiasm for roses ... and these are particularly fine specimens.' He turned to Antonia, greeting her with his usual courtesy and she granted him a careless nod which brought faint colour to his face. 'Just a few roses for your mother,' he said awkwardly, for the beautiful but slightly disdainful girl always made him feel embarrassed and uncomfortable and he sensed that she disliked and resented his attentions to her mother.

'So I see,' she returned indifferently. 'But should you rob the vicar's garden for ours, Commander?'

He was taken aback for it had not occurred to him that his desire to please Eva Standen could expose him to that sneering accusation.

Guy said quietly but with a faint edge to his tone: 'I'm afraid you are not used to Antonia's sense of humour, Commander. We all know that the Vicar would part with all he possesses if it brought pleasure to others.'

The Commander looked anxiously at Eva. 'I should have explained that James sent you the roses with his compliments, my dear ... I mustn't claim the credit for a gift that isn't mine, you know.'

She smiled at him reassuringly. 'But the thought was yours, Arthur dear ... and it is always the thought that one really appreciates.' She turned to her daughter. 'Antonia, do find Sally and ask her to bring a fresh pot of tea—and tell her to make it strong.' She smiled at the Commander. 'Naval men always like strong tea, don't they, Arthur?'

He agreed absently, startled and delighted

41

by the unexpected use of his first name and wondering if she would ever allow him to call her Eva ... and if he dared to suggest it. He was a shy man for all his bluff exterior and in all the months that he had received unmistakable encouragement in his courtship of the gentle, good-natured widow he had never presumed to believe that his affection might be returned.

But the tenderness with which she spoke his name, the haste with which she sought to apply balm to the wound that her daughter had inflicted, and the warm affection in her smile as she turned to him sent his hopes of happiness flying high.

She went on warmly: 'When you've had your tea perhaps we can plant the roses together ... they ought to go in as soon as possible if you can spare the time, Arthur.'

'My time is entirely at your disposal,' he said with old-fashioned gallantry.

'Then we shall enjoy ourselves debating the respective merits of soil and compost and position,' she said gaily. 'I've yet to discover that two gardeners ever share the same views ... perhaps you will surprise me.'

Antonia welcomed the opportunity to escape for she considered the courtship between the elderly naval man and her mother highly amusing. She did not actively dislike the Commander, but his lack of subtlety and oddly boyish awkwardness invited her scorn and she could not imagine that her mother might not gain a great deal of private amusement from the attentions and heavy-handed gallantry of her elderly admirer. She certainly did not suppose that her mother felt any real affection for the Commander or encouraged him with any real aim but to give the lonely old man some interest in life.

She passed on the message to Sally and wandered into the sitting-room, not at all disposed to return to the terrace and play an unnecessary part in entertaining the Commander. Guy glanced into the room and paused in his way to the study for the jar of tobacco that he kept for those of his guests who smoked a pipe.

Antonia looked up from her magazine ... and her eyes began to dance with mischievous amusement. 'How tactful of you not to play gooseberry,' she said lightly.

He smiled. 'Yes, I know,' he said in appreciative understanding of her amusement. 'But Eva likes him ... in fact, I believe she is very fond of him.'

'Oh, nonsense!' she declared. 'She just enjoys having a man in tow ... like all women! I've nothing to say against that ... I merely deplore her taste, that's all.'

'I suppose his approach seems ridiculously old-fashioned to you but Eva is his contemporary, you know.'

'She is still young enough to be flattered by his admiration, of course ... I appreciate that. But does he have to be quite so obvious, Guy ... or so determined to overcome an instinctive nervousness of the opposite sex?'

'He has never married,' Guy reminded her carelessly. 'I imagine he has had very little experience of women ... and Eva seems to have bowled him over completely.'

'She *flirts* with him ... quite outrageously!' Antonia subsided into laughter.

Guy chuckled softly. 'I expect she feels he needs the occasional push, you know. But one is never too old to enjoy a flirtation, Antonia.'

'Does he ever call without bringing some little gift?' she asked curiously.

'No, I don't think so ... why?'

'It seems so ... so Victorian,' she gurgled. 'Acceptable little gifts for the little lady who has won his heart ... handkerchiefs, chocolates, perfume, flowers—could you imagine him presenting Eva with a chiffon nightie or something equally scandalous?'

Guy smiled in response to her laughing words. But he said quietly: 'I wish you wouldn't sneer, Antonia ... he's a dear old boy with a kind heart—and love is no respecter of age, you know.'

She stared at him, startled and incredulous. 'Love? For heaven's sake, Guy

... you surely don't credit him with being in love!'

'Certainly I do. Eventually he will muster sufficient courage to ask Eva to marry him ... and I think it will be an excellent thing for them both. You are too young to know that love need not always be a tempestuous and passionate business, stirring the senses as much as the emotions.'

She said impatiently: 'Oh, Eva wouldn't think of marrying anyone ... no one could replace my father! But if she did she would not choose to marry the Commander ... she could do very much better for herself!' She frowned, thoughtful and a little perturbed. 'I hope she can steel herself to say no if he does ask her, Guy ... you know how soft-hearted she is!'

'He will ask ... and she will accept him very willingly,' he returned quietly. 'And I shall be sincerely pleased for them both, Antonia. The Commander needs someone to protect ... and Eva needs to be protected. I'm afraid she has been very lonely during the last two years.'

'Lonely!' she exclaimed, a little indignant. 'But I have been here ... and you have done all you could to make her content.'

'You are too impatient with her natural interest and concern for you ... and you lead your own life without giving much thought to Eva, I'm afraid. As for myself ... well, I

45

can scarcely provide her with the happiness and security that the Commander can offer. I daresay you haven't noticed that she looks much younger and much prettier these last few months ... since she met the Commander.'

'I hope you are wrong ... because I hate the very thought!' she exclaimed passionately. 'That old man ... and *Eva*! It's disgusting!'

His eyes hardened abruptly and he looked at her with cold dislike. He was angry ... and inwardly she quailed a little. For he never lost his temper as she did so easily ... his anger was slow to stir but icy and implacable when it was invoked. He did not forgive nor forget very readily and Antonia always felt that he regarded her with a faint disappointment after a quarrel. It was not that he brought up past quarrels or heaped recriminations on her head when the heat of the battle was over ... he seldom referred to their angry exchanges except with a hint of regret. But Antonia was impulsive and quick-tempered and the hasty words that flew to her lips when they quarrelled were often regretted almost immediately ... and it was dismaying to realise that they had left a lasting impression on Guy for she was not as indifferent to his good opinion as she pretended.

'Guard your tongue!' he said coldly. 'You

always were and always will be utterly self-centred and insensitive. You are behaving like a spoilt and jealous child!'

'Jealous!' She gave an infuriated little laugh. 'Don't be absurd!'

'Of course you are jealous,' he said quietly, sternly. 'Partly on your father's behalf, I suppose—which is very misguided of you for Philip always hoped that Eva might find happiness a second time if anything happened to him. But mainly on your own behalf, Antonia ... because you must always be of prior importance to the people in your life even though you are incapable of caring anything for them in return.'

Shocked and furious, almost beside herself with rage, she slapped him full in the face. 'How *dare* you ...!' she choked, almost too angry to voice the words.

He caught her wrist in a steely grip and their eyes met and held in fierce and angry challenge. 'Don't ever do that again,' he said softly, so softly that she barely caught the words. She drew back in instinctive alarm. The marks of her fingers stood out in faint red weals on his cheek and his eyes were smouldering with a passionate and yet oddly despairing anger.

She struggled to free herself, trembling from head to foot with the violence of her emotions, hating him with an intensity that shocked her and yet wishing with all her

47

heart that she had not dealt him that insulting blow. She was very near to tears ... but pride kept them at bay.

'You're hurting me!' she stormed. 'You despicable brute ... oh, how I *hate* you, Guy Carlow!'

That faintly sardonic smile briefly touched his lips. 'Because I'm the only man who knows you for what you really are ... a shrew and a vixen, determined to take what you want in life at all costs, determined to go your own way without a thought for anyone else! Because I'm not taken in by your pretty face and empty charm! Because I dare to tell you the truth about yourself ... and you don't like to hear it! Of course you hate me ... it would be surprising if you didn't, my dear.' He released her wrist almost contemptuously and she moved away from him swiftly, rubbing the chafed skin, throwing him a vicious glance. 'I'm afraid I hurt you,' he said mildly. 'But violence breeds violence, you know, Antonia.'

He went quietly from the room without a backward glance ... and she threw herself on the settee as the tears welled and overflowed. They were tears of temper and mortification ... but the unhappiness which seemed to engulf her entire being was rooted in the oddly dismaying conviction that he utterly despised her...

It was just as though she experienced the

bitter taste of rejection by a man whose liking and admiration and affection she had always valued more than she had known ... and Antonia was bewildered and disturbed and confused and shocked—and even vaguely resentful that she had not realised before the need to tread warily where Guy was concerned.

She thought despairingly that she had been so intent on disliking and despising him, so intent on emphasising her complete indifference to him, that it had simply never occurred to her that it might be painful to discover that his loathing and contempt matched her own. Liking and affection and interest and attention had all come her way so easily throughout her life that she had automatically assumed that she could behave as badly as she pleased to any man and still lift a finger to bring him to her side, eager and adoring. How stupid she had been to deceive herself that if it had crossed her mind to want Guy Carlow she could have had him for the wishing!

Had she really always imagined that he cared for her behind that mask of serene and careless indifference? Had she really supposed that she was punishing him for the hurt and humiliation he had inflicted on her, all those years ago, by flaunting her interest in other men and spurning all that he would offer if she gave him the right amount of encouragement?

She was appalled to realise her own conceit for all unconsciously she *had* assumed that he cared for her but had not chosen to allow a seventeen year old girl to know that she had conquered a mature and experienced man with her loveliness and charm and warm personality. And she had assumed that his failure to marry any other woman stemmed from his continued love for her and the hope he would never admit that one day she might marry him.

She was suddenly aware of the truth with a blinding, frightening clarity ... and with it came the astonishing discovery that she had always wanted Guy's affection and understanding, his admiration and respect ... the warmth and tenderness and sweet security of being loved by such a man. But she had been too proud, too stubborn to admit it, nursing her grudge against him without even questioning why it should still matter so much that a man she despised had scorned the offer of her youthful, immature, impulsive love for him. She had utterly convinced herself that he no longer meant anything to her ... now that she knew beyond a shadow of a doubt that she could never mean anything to Guy, she desperately wanted to mean everything in the world to him!

There were no more tears ... the agony

that consumed her was too great for such easy relief. For she knew that she could not redeem herself in his eyes...

He had told her bluntly that she was a shrew and a vixen, a spoiled and selfish and insensitive child who cared for no one but herself ... and Antonia thought miserably that she could not deny the justice of his accusations. She had swept through life without regard for anything but what she wanted ... and she had used people, taking admiration and affection as her right, giving nothing in return but careless, casual friendship and discarding the men who had briefly interested her without a thought for any pain she inflicted. She had carelessly supposed that her fleeting friendship, a few meaningless kisses, the bestowing of her company, her smiles, her vivacious charm and her fickle affection were sufficient reward for any man who inevitably fell in love with her. She had taken with both hands ... and given nothing that could be valued or remembered in return, she thought bitterly— and did not wonder that Guy, who had never been impressed by her beauty or deceived by her pretence of warm and flattering interest, should fail to love her as other men did.

But had they really loved her ... those men who had briefly played a part in her life? Was it possible that any man could truly love a woman who was so wrapped in selfishness and vanity?

If only Guy could learn to love her, after all! If only she could convince him that she was different, that she had changed, that she wanted nothing more than to belong to him, to love him, to do all she could to secure his happiness and peace of mind and heart! But he would never believe that she loved him ... he would never trust such a sudden volte-face in her feelings ... he would only suppose that, as always, she could not bear to be of no importance to anyone and was endeavouring to charm her way into his affections. It was entirely her own fault that he despised and distrusted her ... but it seemed very hard that she should love him so much and know herself incapable of winning his love in return.

She had not changed after all, she thought despairingly. She still wanted *her* happiness and instinctively sought for ways and means of securing it. She still wanted to be liked and admired, to feel that she was of supreme importance, to know that she inspired love and longing. She still could not endure the thought of rejection ... although for the first time in her life it was her heart and not her pride that was threatened by a man's failure to recognise that she merited his love.

Love was supposed to be the longing to give—and to go on giving. So why did she want so desperately to receive love in return

... why was it simply not enough to love Guy and to want his happiness more than her own? Why was it so impossible to believe that he could find any happiness in life without her? It seemed that loving was involved with just as many selfish desires and just as much vanity as not loving, she thought wearily ... but it did not occur to her to doubt that she loved Guy. For every instinct, every fibre of her being, every throb of her heart acclaimed her new awareness of all that he meant to her ... all that he must always mean to her...

CHAPTER FIVE

Antonia drove the sleek, scarlet car at a much more leisurely pace than usual for her thoughts were busy and she could not afford to take chances on the traffic-laden arterial road.

She was on her way back to town, back to the familiar security of the friends and the way of life that she knew and understood. For she felt that the ground had vanished beneath her feet with the sudden discovery of all that Guy meant to her. It was too unexpected, too alarming ... for she had never imagined that she would find herself in the position of loving any man who did not love her in return. So many men had found it easy to love her ... but she had never felt anything more for any of them than a mild affection or a ridiculous, short-lived infatuation. Now she knew what it meant to love ... and knew all the despair and heartache of loving in vain.

Guy would suppose that she had rushed away rather than face him again after quarrelling with him so violently ... and it was true. But it was not the quarrel which had urged her to escape so precipitately. She had felt that she could not stay beneath his roof, knowing that she loved him, knowing that he despised her ... she had felt that she needed time to marshal her thoughts and emotions before she met him again.

She needed to come to terms with this new-found loving that was so much more demanding, so much more devastating, than the foolish, immature infatuation she had experienced when she was seventeen. She was still faintly incredulous, faintly dismayed, faintly shocked by the realisation of all that Guy abruptly meant to her life ... and she did not know how to cope with all the emotional turbulence of her feelings. She did not know what she could have said to him, how she could have behaved towards him, if they had met again too soon ... and she had been terrified of betraying her need for a man whose disbelief and mockery and indifference would hurt and humiliate her beyond bearing.

She had slipped away without a word to anyone, thankful for the Commander's presence which absorbed her mother's attention so completely as they busied themselves with planting the roses ... for she had known that she must not risk the swift and intuitive perception that Eva had always shown where she was concerned.

Thinking of her mother and of the Commander, Antonia felt a pang of envy for the simplicity of their regard for each other ... and realised that she had accepted not only the likelihood of marriage between them but also her mother's right to find happiness for the second time if she could. She knew that she had often embarrassed the Commander and distressed her mother by her attitude to their friendship ... and she regretted it now. Not only because she had confirmed Guy's poor opinion of her but also because she must have caused unnecessary pain ... and there was quite enough pain in loving without adding to it, she thought unhappily. Awareness of her own feelings had abruptly made her much more sensitive to those of other people ... and although she still found it difficult to accept that a man approaching sixty might be in love she was prepared to consider that there might be many kinds of loving.

It had not been easy for Antonia, so used to supposing herself all that any man could want, so used to the easy admiration and undemanding friendship and careless acceptance of those who did not look beyond her beauty and her natural charm, to face the truth in Guy's accusations, to admit with shame and regret that she had been selfish and vain and intent on securing her own desires in all things and both insensitive and indifferent to the thoughts and feelings of others. But she had the courage to admit her failings ... and the strength of character to determine that she would be a different person in the future.

It was unlikely that Guy could be brought to think more kindly of her or that he would place much trust in her change of heart. But she was beginning to realise that it was more important than she had supposed to be respected and liked and admired for one's good qualities rather than because one had chanced to be born with good looks and charm of manner. She was beginning to understand why Guy deplored those friends who lived only for the moment with little kindness or consideration or compassion or interest for anyone who did not conform to their way of living. She was beginning to feel that there was a brittle emptiness in the eternal pursuit of pleasure and very little satisfaction in having no one but herself to consider or to please.

She felt a little out of her depth, knowing that she wanted a new and more rewarding way of life but needing someone to guide her in the right direction. How did one change a way of life overnight? Did she have sufficient courage to risk the amusement and faint scorn of her friends? It was all very well to tell herself that their friendship was of very little value, that she could always make new friends ... but how did one begin?

She booked in at a hotel for the night for she had not yet made up her mind what she was going to do. She had thrown an assortment of clothes and shoes into a case without any coherent thought for the immediate future except that she could no longer continue to accept Guy's hospitality. It would be quite difficult enough to meet him from time to time without inviting the hell of living in the same house with his indifference and her own fear of betraying how much she loved him.

It irked her anew that financially she was so dependent on Guy. But he could not compel her to live in his house and if he still refused to pay the rent of a flat then she would simply have to find the money out of her allowance...

She did not think he could want her beneath his roof now that she had alienated him completely with that impulsive and much-regretted blow. And nothing on earth could persuade her to return to Mersleigh End! Hotels were expensive ... but perhaps she could share Evelyn's flat until she found a place of her own. Evelyn was a good-natured girl and she would not object ... but if she intended to break with that particular set it must not be too long before she found somewhere else to live!

Alone in the quiet, comfortable but utterly impersonal hotel room, Antonia felt she could not bear the sense of desolation which swept over her. She had never felt so lonely in all her life ... or so desperately in need of reassurance.

Impulsively she reached out to the telephone, all her fine thoughts and resolutions brushed to one side in the need for the company of someone who did not loathe and despise her and think her completely beyond the pale...

Leo was home and pleased by her call ... and more surprised than he chose to convey. For it was the first time that she had voluntarily sought his company ... and he wondered what had urged the proud and elusive and very lovely Antonia to offer so much encouragement.

He had never pursued any woman for so long without reward ... but he had never experienced the least difficulty in persuading women to fall in love with him—until he met

Antonia Standen. She did not show the least inclination to love him and he frequently felt with some chagrin that she was more amused than flattered by his attentions. He often wondered why she encouraged him at all when she was so swift to suppress any attempt on his part to introduce a more intimate note into their relationship. But he rather suspected that she was enjoying her doubtful victory over the other women who sought to attract him and failed because his thoughts and emotions and desires had been centred on Antonia Standen since their first meeting.

He could not quite analyse her appeal for him ... obviously physical in part and yet there was much more to his feeling for Antonia than mere physical attraction. She was not like the other women he had known ... and it was not only because she had not fallen an easy victim to his good looks and practised charm.

She was a 'good girl,' he thought wryly as he replaced the receiver, having promised to call for her in half an hour and take her out to dinner ... and the old-fashioned term did not wholly apply to that puritan streak in her make-up. He had made the easy mistake of judging her by her friends, by her way of life, by her seemingly reckless approach to life ... but having known her for some months he knew that she was not cast in the same mould, that she was merely drifting with the tide because she had no incentive to change direction ... and he smiled with faint self-mockery at the whimsical thought that she was like a ship without a waiting harbour. She was insecure ... and he suspected that at some time she had been badly hurt and had plunged into a reckless, extravagant, aimless way of life in a desperate attempt to conceal her hurt from the world. The way of life had become a habit, something she did not really know how to escape from although she was neither happy nor any more secure.

He supposed it was that knowledge and her youth that made him feel oddly protective towards her and maintained his interest long after the same attitude she adopted in another woman would have caused him to shrug his shoulders and turn away.

He wanted her more than he had ever wanted any other woman ... and no doubt his desire was the greater because he knew it did not meet with any response. She was not cold but merely unawakened, he thought ruefully ... and it seemed that he was not the man to stir her sleeping senses to leaping life.

He could not even believe that her elusiveness was aimed at the acquisition of a wedding ring. It was an ancient and familiar strategy but he did not think it had ever crossed her mind. She did not want to marry him ... and her elusiveness was apparently born of an indifference that was a constant challenge and a disappointment.

As he made his way across the city towards her hotel, Leo wished it were possible to cut her out of his life and forget all about her. But it was not possible. For he was very near to loving Antonia Standen as he had never loved any woman. Certainly he had never wished before that he had more to offer a woman than a name that had been dragged through the divorce courts on innumerable occasions! Antonia would never marry him ... for she would not believe that he would never want any other woman if she were his wife ... and, although he was sincere in wishing to marry her, he could scarcely believe it himself!

Antonia took pains with her appearance, anxious to conceal any tell-tale signs of her inner turmoil. She stared at her reflection in the mirror with a faint surprise that she looked exactly the same as usual. Perhaps she was a little pale and there was just a hint of strain in her eyes. But a casual observer would not notice those things. She had half expected that the abrupt alteration in her outlook on love and life must show itself in her face ... that anyone who looked at her must know immediately that she had been stirred to the depths of her being by the

61

belated realisation that she loved Guy. But there was nothing to indicate to Leo that she had called him only because she was desperately lonely and sick at heart and she had known with comforting certainty that he would come in response to her call.

She realised all the dangers of turning to a man like Leo for comfort, but there was also a certain safety in encouraging a man who did not mean to fall in love with her and would not expect her to fall in love with him. Their relationship had always been light and easy and undemanding because she had been determined that it should be ... and it was all that she felt she could handle just now.

She struggled to convince herself that his interest and admiration and attentions would ease her heartache. He was attractive and amusing, after all ... and she could not spend her life in painful longing for a man who did not want her. Perhaps in time the ache in her heart would lessen ... perhaps in time she would recover from this violent and unexpected attack of love and find it possible to welcome the attentions of other men, even to love again.

Leo was waiting in the cocktail lounge when she went down ... and she went to join him at the bar, oddly unconscious of the stirring of admiration that her appearance evoked. He turned, smiling, his eyes warming to her beauty and her slender, youthful grace ... and he felt a stirring of dismay and compassion as he recognised the bleakness in the beautiful eyes that her answering smile could not disguise.

'You look very lovely,' he murmured as she slipped on to the stool by his side.

She smiled ... and still it was merely a curving of the lips. 'Thank you for coming,' she said quietly. 'I scarcely expected to find you at home.'

'We were supposed to meet at Evelyn's for cocktails,' he reminded her gently. 'I'd just returned from her flat when you telephoned.'

She looked at him in faint dismay. 'I'm sorry ... I forgot all about it, Leo.'

He smiled, a little wryly. Women did not usually forget their appointments with him ... and he was a little surprised to discover that he was still capable of being hurt by a woman. But Antonia was a very different type of woman to those he had known in the past. 'It doesn't matter,' he said lightly. He smiled down at her with a tenderness that she did not even notice in his blue eyes. 'I'm glad you called me, anyway.'

Antonia sipped her cocktail and glanced without interest about the room. 'This is a dreary place,' she said critically. 'Why are hotels always so respectable?'

He chuckled. 'You don't care for respectability?'

'It's so dull, isn't it?' she returned brightly.

'Definitely dull,' he agreed. 'This is the kind of place that always cramps my style.' He reached for her slender fingers. 'Why don't we have a quiet dinner at my flat?' he suggested lightly ... and with no other thought in mind but the desire to discover what it was that troubled her and to comfort her a little if he could.

She withdrew her hand. 'Because I want to visit that new nightclub ... *The Inferno,*' she returned smoothly. 'I'm told that it has a very interesting cabaret.'

He should have expected the rebuff, he thought ruefully ... his reputation was no advantage at all where Antonia was concerned. But he could not resist leaning towards her to murmur in her ear, his eyes twinkling: 'Why not allow me to provide the interest, my sweet?'

She moved away slightly. 'Do behave,' she said irritably. 'I'm not in the mood, Leo.'

Few women responded to his advances with just that note of impatience ... and for a moment he was piqued and exasperated and very ready to end the futile pursuit of the lovely and elusive Antonia.

She glanced at him briefly ... and surprised an expression in his blue eyes that she had never seen before. Her own eyes widened a little for it had never occurred to her that Leo could be hurt or dismayed by anything she said or did ... for she had never supposed that she meant any more to him than a possible conquest. His persistence in the light of her careless acceptance of his attentions had never seemed puzzling until that moment ... but she wondered with a slight sense of shock if his interest was more serious than she had imagined.

She was oddly sensitive to his feelings ... and she did not wholly welcome the stirring of regret. Her heart was heavy enough without the additional burden of compassion for others. But she had not intended nor expected to hurt him with her impatient rebuff ... and she was sorry that she had brought that fleeting pain to his eyes.

She smiled at him ... and her smile was enchanting when it touched her eyes, warm and generous and very sweet. 'I'm sorry, Leo,' she said impulsively. 'I've had a trying afternoon. Can you bear with me ... or shall we just have a drink and forget about dinner? I'm really not fit company for anyone tonight.'

'What's wrong?' he asked gently.

She shrugged briefly. 'I've been home ...' she said, as though that was sufficient explanation.

And it was ... for Leo knew and understood her resentment of Guy Carlow and the circumstances which gave the man a certain authority over her actions and behaviour. It was very natural that she should resent it ... and equally natural that a beautiful and much-admired woman should resent the attitude of a man who seemed to regard her as little more than an inconvenience in his life. Realising that there had been another quarrel between them, he was immediately indignant on Antonia's behalf ... and immediately determined to do all he could to erase the unpleasantness of the afternoon from her thoughts.

'Then you definitely need a little gaiety to raise your spirits,' he said firmly. 'Finish your drink and I'll take you to *The Inferno*, my sweet.'

It was not his fault that she did not enjoy the evening. He was quietly attentive, swift to anticipate her wishes, gentle and considerate and sensitive to her mood ... and she appreciated his determination to keep the evening on a light and unemotional basis. She had never liked him so well ... and almost wished she had chosen to fall in love with a man who regarded her with admiration and affection rather than with Guy who left her in no doubt as to his contemptuous indifference. But she had not *chosen* to fall in love with him, she thought miserably ... it had just happened!

CHAPTER SIX

Eva was anxious. It was not at all unusual for Antonia to leave the house without a word to anyone and she frequently stayed with friends for a few days. But it was almost a week since she had taken her car and more of her clothes than she could possibly need for a brief stay in town ... and there had been neither a letter nor a telephone call to tell them of her whereabouts.

Perhaps she was worrying unnecessarily ... Antonia was often careless about informing them of her intentions and no doubt she would return home in a day or two, bubbling over with all that she had been doing and quite surprised to discover that she had forgotten to explain her acceptance of an invitation or her sudden impulse to visit a particular place or country.

But it was not only Antonia's behaviour that caused Eva so much anxiety. There was also Guy who had been strangely unlike himself all the week ... and this fact, combined with Antonia's sudden departure, convinced her that there had been another and much more bitter quarrel between them.

Guy had been very quiet, very withdrawn, spending most of his time in the study or out with the dogs in the warm sunshine that had continued to smile on the countryside, seeming to avoid any company but his own—and although this behaviour could easily be explained by a preoccupation with the new book which might not be going very well, Eva thought it very likely that he was worried about Antonia and might even feel he was to blame for the quarrel which had sent her from the house in such haste.

She hesitated to question him ... and he had not commented on Antonia's departure except to remark that she had always been thoughtless and impulsive and he had ceased to wonder at anything she did. This had been said so coldly that Eva had been surprised and dismayed ... and quite content to accept a change of subject. But she was anxious enough to need reassurance and Guy had always provided it in the past.

She glanced through the pile of letters by her plate. Then she looked across the breakfast table at Guy. He looked tired and rather grim and she wondered if he were sleeping badly. 'Still no news from Antonia ... you haven't had a letter, I suppose?' She allowed a hint of disappointment, a hint of her anxiety to touch the words.

For a moment, Guy was silent as the name wrenched at his heart. He was equally as anxious about Antonia ... but for very different reasons. He did not doubt that she was safe and well and probably staying with friends until she felt she could face him with some degree of composure. He only feared that she would obey some reckless, dangerous impulse in an attempt to punish him in some way for the truths he had thrown at her head ... and she was not likely to pause to consider whether or not she had the power to hurt him by anything she did.

Then he said lightly, carelessly: 'Does Antonia ever write letters? Not to me, certainly!' But he took up his own letters and glanced through them, suddenly shaken by the thought that if Antonia had committed the folly that he had imagined too many times during the last week she would probably break the news to him in a formal letter. He shook his head, knowing a relief that he did not betray by expression or tone as he said: 'No, I'm afraid my mail is mostly comprised of bills.'

'It's almost a week,' Eva said quietly.

'I suppose it must be,' he replied with convincing indifference. 'You are not worried, surely? She has been away from home for much longer periods, Eva.'

'Not without letting me know where she is,' she returned firmly.

He smiled suddenly, warmly. 'Why not enjoy the brief respite? She will soon be home and cutting up your peace of mind, you know.'

She laughed reluctantly. 'Oh, I do know

... but she is my daughter, Guy. I like to know where she is and what she is doing.'

'So do I,' he said wryly. 'I shudder to think of the bills she is probably running up in revenge for the cancellation of that damned car!'

Her eyes rested on his face thoughtfully. 'Was it worth it, Guy?' she asked gently.

'I hope so,' he said, a little grimly. 'I don't care what money she spends ... but I do dislike her attitude, Eva.'

'It's such a pity that you can't be friends,' she sighed. 'So much unpleasantness...'

'Yes ... it is a pity,' he agreed quietly. He stretched out a hand to cover her own in swift and affectionate reassurance. 'But she shouldn't allow you to be anxious about her ... shall I scold her for you when she does come home?' he suggested lightly, warmly.

'Oh, no!' she said hastily.

He smiled. 'You think she might rush away again? Perhaps you're right ... and while I appreciate the serenity of life without her I do prefer to have her beneath my roof, you know.'

'I'm afraid you dislike it all very much,' Eva said with all the impulsiveness that she had passed on to her daughter. 'She *is* difficult, I know ... but she is so young and terribly sensitive, Guy.'

He nodded. 'She is certainly young ... but I don't think she is particularly sensitive about quarrelling with me, my dear. She has probably forgotten the incident ... and is much too involved with her friends to realise that we might be anxious about her. She remembered an appointment and rushed away to keep it ... and probably imagines that she told us her plans for the rest of the week. We should have heard soon enough if anything had happened to her, you know,' he added gently.

'Yes ... of course,' she agreed quickly, rising from the table and picking up her letters. She hesitated and then said tentatively: 'You're going into town today, aren't you, Guy?'

'Yes. I'm meeting Ames this morning and will probably lunch with him.' That warm and attractive smile lurked in his eyes as he looked at her with perfect understanding. 'Would you like me to contact some of Antonia's friends and find out where she is if I can?' he asked lightly.

Her eyes brightened swiftly. 'Would you?'

'Certainly ... if it will set your mind at rest,' he said carelessly ... and Eva went from the room wondering that he should find it necessary to pretend an unconcern that his manner in the past days had certainly not indicated.

Guy's lips twisted a little wryly as the door closed behind Eva. He could not allow her to be anxious about Antonia without doing what he could to reassure her ... but he did not relish the task he had set himself. No doubt it would be a very simple business to discover Antonia's present whereabouts but he was very reluctant to give the impression that he was concerned or even interested by her sudden departure and prolonged absence. He did not wonder why Eva had failed to contact her daughter's friends ... she was a little nervous of Antonia's quick temper and fierce resentment of any undue curiosity as to her affairs.

Before he left for town, he telephoned Evelyn Hurst who was one of Antonia's more acceptable friends. He learned without surprise that Antonia was staying with Evelyn but had just left the flat to meet Leo Bryce.

'Is it important, Guy?' Evelyn asked, curiosity touching her voice. 'Shall I ask her to call you when she comes back?'

'Thank you ... but it isn't important. I shall be in town today and merely wondered if she cared to meet me for lunch.'

'Oh ... I imagine she means to lunch with Leo,' Evelyn said cheerfully.

'Very likely,' he returned carelessly and rang off after exchanging a few polite pleasantries. He realised that Evelyn would certainly mention his call to Antonia but that could not be helped ... he had found out what he wanted to know and could assure

Eva that her daughter was safe and well and following her usual pursuit of pleasure.

Eva received the news with obvious relief but she glanced up at him with a puzzled look in her eyes. 'Don't you think it's a little odd that she hasn't even telephoned, Guy?'

He thought it extremely thoughtless and irresponsible behaviour but he merely said lightly: 'Not at all. She hasn't a thought in her head for anyone but herself, you know.'

'I suppose not.' She sighed. 'If only Philip hadn't indulged her so much ... but she was such a sweet little girl. Everyone thought her quite adorable.'

'Including Antonia herself,' he said drily. 'It's a pity she's too old to have her bottom smacked ... it would do her the world of good.'

Eva's sense of the ridiculous betrayed her in a faint chuckle. But she said, a little wistfully: 'Perhaps you'll see her in town, Guy ... and then you can ask her when she means to come home.'

'If Antonia and I meet I shall very likely wring her lovely neck,' he said, smiling ... but there was steel behind the words and Eva looked after him with faint apprehension in her eyes as he strode towards his car...

The quiet, conventional grey saloon covered the twenty-two miles into London in a little over an hour. Guy drove well and carefully, always alert for the unexpected,

73

swift to anticipate the actions of other motorists, cool and capable in his handling of the car. But one part of his mind remained with Antonia for she had been too much in his thoughts during the past week to be easily dismissed.

With that angry blow, she had struck at a very vulnerable part of his being ... his pride. He had forgiven her a great many things in the last few years ... but he could not forgive her for striking him. Even more than his pride, she had plunged a knife into his heart with her venomous declaration of hatred that had carried so much force of feeling. Making as many allowances as he could for that ungovernable temper, for the provocation, for the impulsiveness which had always touched her speech as well as her behaviour, it was still painfully obvious that she detested him ... and he had struggled for days between a fierce, proud, angry desire to put her out of his heart and the bitter knowledge that he had loved her too long and too deeply for his feelings to change in any way. His love and his longing and his desire to keep her by his side for the rest of his life was too much a part of him ... no matter how she hurt him, he must always love her. But his pride would smart for a long time at the memory of her forceful hand on his cheek ... and his heart was still angry for all its loving.

He had long ceased to wonder why he

should love Antonia of all the women in the world. He simply accepted that she was the woman he had been destined to love and to need. He had known her in every mood, knew all her failings, frequently felt that it was too late for Antonia to alter ... and yet he knew instinctively that for all her faults she could become a warm, sweet and generous woman, utterly lovable, utterly necessary to a man's happiness and well-being. She only needed to fall in love ... deeply and irrevocably in love. She must be capable of such loving ... if only he knew the way to her heart!

Ames Sinclair was an old friend as well as his publisher and they had a great deal to discuss. Business matters completed and set aside, they turned to more personal subjects ... and there was still much to talk about when they eventually adjourned to a well-known restaurant for lunch.

They were scarcely settled in their seats when a faint murmur of interest and admiration rippled around the room. Guy did not glance up from the menu but Ames turned in his seat and said immediately and with delight: 'Why, it's Antonia!'

Guy glanced across the room with seeming indifference ... but he had been jolted by the words. She looked very lovely, very self-possessed—and anger stirred anew as she smiled at Leo Bryce who was escorting her to their table with a light hand at her elbow. They were a striking couple and it seemed that they were drawing attention from every corner of the big room. She sat down, glancing carelessly about the room ... so carelessly that she did not appear to notice him, Guy thought—and did not doubt that she had seen him. Their eyes met briefly across the tables ... then she turned away to speak to Bryce. The man bent over her to speak before he took his own seat ... and there was a warmth in his eyes that caused Guy to raise an eyebrow in faint surprise. Abruptly it occurred to him that Bryce might be more dangerous than he had supposed ... it certainly appeared that there was more to that friendship than he could wish.

Having sought in vain to catch her eye, Ames turned back to his friend. 'She's a beautiful girl, Guy,' he said quietly.

Guy nodded. 'Very beautiful,' he said drily.

Ames glanced at him with faint reproach. He was no stranger to their mutual antagonism but he often felt that Guy did not make sufficient allowance for Antonia's youth and popularity. She might be a little wild, a little wilful ... but there was no real harm in the girl. She needed a firm but tender hand on her rein ... and momentarily Ames found himself wishing that he were not a married man.

Guy smiled sardonically. 'Antonia is drawn to the Bryces in this world, old man,' he said lightly. 'But you are much better off with Alicia, you know.'

Ames threw him an indignant glance. But, meeting Guy's twinkling eyes, he laughed a little ruefully. 'I expect she thinks I'm a dull dog!'

'Nonsense ... Alicia adores you,' Guy assured him smoothly.

Ames laughed again. 'You know perfectly well I was speaking of Antonia.'

'Yes ... well, she thinks I'm a dull dog, too,' he said comfortingly, mischief lurking in his dark eyes. 'We're the wrong side of thirty, Ames.'

Ames leaped to the bait. 'Bryce must be all of thirty-five.'

'Then perhaps we *are* dull dogs and not merely too old for her,' Guy said, smiling.

Ames turned to look at Antonia and her companion. Heads together, they were studying the menu ... and she seemed to be oblivious of everyone else in the room. 'That affair has lasted longer than I expected,' he said quietly.

'Longer than anyone expected, I imagine,' Guy returned drily.

'Bryce appears to be very fond of her,' Ames commented.

'Antonia has a great talent for inspiring affection in almost everyone she knows,' he said carelessly.

'Shouldn't we draw attention to ourselves,' Ames suggested, a little eagerly. Guy made no response. 'One doesn't like to intrude, I suppose,' he went on reluctantly.

'Then we won't,' Guy said lightly. 'Come ... what will you eat, Ames? Or has your healthy appetite vanished with your lost youth?'

Ames grinned and took the proffered menu. 'I haven't seen Antonia for some months,' he said as though he felt some explanation for his interest was demanded.

'I would gladly change places with you,' Guy returned with a smile that took the sting from the words.

During the meal he contrived to keep Ames' attention from straying too frequently ... but he was not surprised when his friend said, almost abruptly: 'Perhaps they would like to join us for coffee.'

Guy smiled faintly. 'I don't think Bryce would thank you for the suggestion ... nor Antonia, for that matter. I am not one of her favourite people just now.'

'I see ...' Ames said in perfect understanding.

It had puzzled him that Antonia seemed quite determined not to look in their direction ... and that she could be quite so oblivious of their presence when they were separated by only a few tables. Now he realised that she was aware of their presence and reluctant to be drawn into the necessary recognition and inevitable contact. Another quarrel, he thought ruefully ... and they were both such proud and stubborn characters! 'It's an unfortunate business,' he said sympathetically. 'It must be very difficult for you both at times.'

Guy shrugged ... a gesture that implied supreme indifference. 'Only when Antonia chooses to make it difficult.'

Ames grinned and scrawled his name across the bill. Then he pushed back his chair. 'Come along, St. Guy ... and at the risk of inviting your wrath I mean to speak to Antonia. I'm afraid I haven't the courage to pass her without a word.'

'I mean to speak to her myself,' Guy told him lightly. 'And if there's an ounce of justice in this world she should blush to the roots of her hair, the little baggage!'

CHAPTER SEVEN

Antonia did not know that he was hoping for the heat of discomfiture to flood into her lovely face. She only knew that the blood seemed to drain from her cheeks as she met Guy's dark, inscrutable eyes.

Her heart had faltered at first sight of him

... and then he had glanced towards her with so much indifference, so much cold disdain in his expression that pride had leaped to quell her trembling heart. She had forced herself to smile, to talk, to toy with some pretence of appetite with the food that Leo had ordered with particular attention to her likes and dislikes. She had struggled to still the pounding of her heart, the longing to turn her glance again and again to the table where Guy sat in such studied indifference to her presence ... and she had succeeded only by constantly reminding herself of the last time that they had met, the things he had said to her and the unmistakable contempt and loathing in his attitude.

It helped that Ames was with him ... and she was grateful for his light, admiring and friendly approach—and for the necessity to introduce the two men who had not met before. Guy was silent, his eyes on her face ... and against her will she was drawn to look at him once more.

She could never be sure of the thoughts behind the faintly mocking expression of his dark eyes ... that sardonic and exasperating smile that lingered about his lips conveyed nothing.

She said, rather lamely: 'I didn't know you meant to be in town today.'

And immediately regretted the words as he said coolly: 'How could you know? We have not been in touch just lately.'

His choice of words seemed a deliberate taunt. But she could not respond with the anger that would have flared so short a time before. 'I ... I meant to write,' she stumbled ... and wished he did not have the power to make her feel like a guilty, awkward schoolgirl. She was thankful that Leo and Ames were talking with the ease and informality of people who had taken a swift and unexpected liking to each other ... and for the moment she and Guy might have been alone in that crowded room.

'The telephone is so much more convenient, don't you think?' he drawled.

Her chin tilted slightly as pride gradually seeped back into her heart. 'I'm staying with Evelyn for the time being ... would you let Eva know? She might be a little worried.' She managed a shaky laugh. 'She is never content unless she is worrying about someone or something, you know.'

'I do know,' he said, a little curtly, stung by the lightness of words and manner. How amused and how amazed she would be to know of the anxiety that had been gnawing at him all the week! Wilful, selfish, egotistical ... she would never alter. 'I am not exactly a stranger, Antonia,' he added drily.

But that was just what he seemed, she thought unhappily ... a cold and forbidding stranger. For all their long antagonism, their hostility to each other, their many quarrels, she had never felt until this moment that an impenetrable barrier stood between them. Fear and dismay touched the very core of her being as she realised that the barrier was of Guy's making and that he would never again attempt to reach a closer understanding with her as he had done so many times in the past only to be rebuffed. She could not hope for any degree of affection or friendship or intimacy in the future where Guy was concerned ... the door had always been open in the past, she realised too late. Now it was firmly closed against her ... he had decided that she no longer merited anything but a necessary, formal courtesy and his reluctant attention to her financial affairs.

She smiled vaguely as if in appreciation of his dry sense of humour—and then she turned to the others, breaking in on their conversation with a faint air of desperation. Guy, hurt and infuriated by her careless insouciance, was deaf to the note of strain in her voice and he construed her interruption as the unconscious rudeness she so often displayed. Wrapped in selfishness, she was frequently impervious to anything that was going on outside her own personal sphere ... she seemed to imagine that the world stood still until she was ready to acknowledge it once more, he thought coldly, deliberately coaxing the fire of his anger against her to fresh life rather than dwell on the sickness of heart caused by her careless indifference...

As soon as courtesy would allow, he drew his reluctant friend from the restaurant—and sensed rather than saw the relief in Antonia's beautiful eyes as she watched them go.

Ames glanced at his friend's set features and thought he had never seen him look so grim. He wondered idly what had passed between Guy and Antonia in that brief exchange. He had never taken their animosity very seriously ... perhaps because Antonia was a creature of moods and Guy was not a man to bear malice. He had often felt that Guy was more inclined to be amused than annoyed by Antonia's fiery temperament ... and no one who had seen her with eyes blazing with fury against Guy only to discover that she was laughing and talking to him in perfect amity the next moment could believe that she really disliked and resented the man who had been her father's friend for so many years. But he was a shrewd and perceptive man ... and he realised that this was no ordinary quarrel. He had not been so interested in talking to Leo Bryce, who might or might not be persuaded to write his autobiography, that he had failed to notice the tension between his friend and the beautiful Antonia. They might have been bitter enemies meeting in temporary and fully armed truce!

The two men parted company outside the restaurant on the issue and acceptance of an invitation to Guy to dine with Ames and his wife the following week. Then Ames set off to walk briskly through the beginning of a downpour to his nearby office to keep the first appointment of the afternoon ... and Guy, with a glance at the overcast skies and the knowledge that the rest of the day was his own and there was nothing to speed his return to Mersleigh End, turned back into the restaurant and made his way to the bar. He ordered a drink and took out his cigarette case and sat watching the rain through the windows and deliberately averting his thoughts from Antonia and Bryce who were no doubt lingering over their coffee in mutual admiration and affection...

As the two men made their way towards the door, Leo glanced at his companion's lovely face ... and he was struck by the haunting sadness which touched her expression. Then he looked down at the slim hand which gripped the stem of her wineglass so fiercely that her taut knuckles gleamed white. He frowned. Was it the unexpected encounter with Carlow that had brought that strange desolation to her eyes, that dismaying tension to her slight body?

She had welcomed Ames Sinclair with warmth and friendliness that had seemed in marked contrast to her cool, almost discourteous reception of Carlow's quiet greeting. Leo wondered in retrospect if it had been a hint of rudeness that he sensed in her manner ... or an unusual lack of self-possession as though she had been taken by surprise. And yet she had not been surprised when the two men paused by their table ... he recalled that she had stiffened slightly in her seat and lost the thread of a remark only a moment or two before so it seemed that she had been conscious and a little apprehensive of their intention.

He had not noticed Carlow until the two men came towards their table ... with Antonia by his side, he found it difficult to concentrate on anything but her lovely face and how much he wanted and needed her, and Carlow might have been at the next table for all he knew—or cared! But he realised belatedly that Antonia must have noticed the man the moment they entered the restaurant ... and her knowledge of his presence had ruined her appetite, he thought wryly.

For all her efforts at gaiety, her lightness of speech and manner, her response and appreciation of his attentions, she had seemed on edge throughout the meal ... and, having been a little on edge himself, he had mistakenly supposed that she sensed and was slightly wary of his mood and his intentions. His mouth twisted with faint bitterness ... for he realised that this was not the moment he had hoped it might be. A proposal of marriage would be most untimely when Antonia was scarcely aware of his existence ... and he was beginning to believe that it would never be anything but unwelcome, in any case.

So much for all his hopes of the past week when she had seemed to offer encouragement, had spent so much of her time in his company, had even allowed him to introduce a slightly warmer note into their relationship and led him to suppose that she might care for him a little...

He sighed, almost wishing that he loved her less than he did.

Antonia turned abruptly. 'I'm sorry, Leo ... what did you say?'

He shook his head. 'I didn't speak, my sweet,' he said lightly ... but his heart was heavy. There would be no point in speaking now, he thought bitterly ... and supposed he was long overdue for the heartache and regret that his enemies had always wished for him, remembering how carelessly he had taken love and given so little in return in the past. For the first time in his life he was deeply and sincerely in love ... and it seemed that Antonia had nothing to give him but a careless affection that he welcomed with a gratitude that astonished him.

Antonia looked at him thoughtfully ... but

she did not really see him for he was obscured by the image in her mind's eye ... the image of a lean, harsh, enigmatic face with eyes that glittered with cold, mocking contempt and a mouth that seemed incapable of warmth and humour and tenderness where she was concerned. The face of the man she loved and would always love even though he deliberately sought to hurt and humiliate her, even though they might always be separated by a cold, forbidding, hostile barrier that all her love and longing could not surmount.

Loneliness seemed to seep into her very soul in that moment as she realised how much she loved the man who would never want her, never cherish her, never love her and keep her safe ... she was suddenly filled with a nameless fear and a strange apprehension gripped her heart so that it seemed to pause and the blood in her veins turned abruptly to ice.

It was exactly as if she had reached for the bottom of a pool in light-hearted confidence ... and suddenly and unexpectedly discovered that there was no bottom as the waters closed hungrily over her head. And in panic and desperation, she instinctively reached for the nearest hand-hold ... and although it chanced to be Leo it could just as easily have been any one of a dozen men that she knew...

Her vision cleared ... and she looked at Leo's handsome face and she warmed to him as she realised the hint of anxiety that blended with the tenderness of his gaze. Dear Leo ... it would be comforting if she could believe that he cared for her, wanted her, would take care of her and teach her to forget the claims of another man on her heart and mind.

She reached out her hand ... and felt his firm, strong fingers close over it. She smiled ... and her eyes were warm and inviting and intoxicating to the man who had never expected to see that particular glow in their depths. She said softly: 'Do you know, I was so sure that you were only waiting for the right moment to say the one thing I want to hear?'

He leaned forward, hope leaping all the more fiercely for its sudden quenching. 'Is it the right moment, Antonia?' he said lightly ... but with urgency behind the words.

Her smile was very sweet ... and it held an unmistakable assurance. 'It's the only moment,' she said ... and with complete and utter truth.

He did not read more into the words than he wished. He lifted her hand to his lips, kissing it with a tender humility that would have amazed all who knew him. 'I love you so much,' he said tensely. 'I want you to marry me, Antonia.'

For a moment she hesitated ... but it was only a moment for loneliness and fear and despair threatened to engulf her once more and she reached out with both hands to the security that he offered. 'Then I will,' she told him, smiling.

His hand gripped hers convulsively. But he searched her lovely eyes intently. 'Are you sure?' he asked quietly. 'Knowing what my life has been in the past ... knowing what people will say?'

She leaned forward to touch her lips to his cheek, completely indifferent to their surroundings. 'I'm sure,' she said, plunging into deep waters but trusting that his arms were strong enough to hold and protect her. 'It's what I want more than anything in the world.' She spoke the truth in that moment ... wanting not the man but the marriage he offered, the security and the protection and the healing balm of knowing herself to be loved...

Smiling, he brought a small velvet box from his pocket. 'I'm an incurable optimist,' he said lightly, opening it to disclose an enormous diamond solitaire that flashed swift fire.

Antonia gave a tiny gasp of mingled surprise and delight. She was too feminine not to react to the beautiful ring ... and she allowed him to slip it on to the third finger of her left hand, resolutely stifling the instinctive protest of her heart. 'It's beautiful ...' she said, twisting her hand so that its many facets sparkled in the light. She looked at him in laughing reproach. 'But supposing I'd turned you down?'

He shrugged. 'It was meant for you, anyway. Beautiful women merit beautiful gifts.' He caught both her hands in his own and held them in an urgent grip. 'You are so beautiful, my darling ... I'm afraid I love you too much. You do mean it—you will marry me?'

'I will marry you,' she said quietly—but there was no joy in her heart.

'Soon?' he urged.

She nodded, smiling at him with tender, indulgent affection. 'Very soon,' she said, still clinging to the only raft in the troubled seas that surrounded her heart and mind...

Leo was too thankful, too filled with gratitude for the promise of a happiness he had supposed it was too late for him to know, to question the love that seemed so abruptly to have taken the place of careless acceptance and near-indifference. He mistook the urgency and eagerness of pain and desperation for the urgency and eagerness of an emotion that matched his own love and longing ... and it was a mistake that was easily made for he swept her along on the tide of his own feelings and Antonia, relieved and grateful, could almost believe that she cared for the man she had promised to marry...

Guy had not been consciously waiting for them to leave the restaurant but he had felt no desire to desert the quiet and comfortable bar for the wet streets. It was only at the moment of their laughing exit that he realised, as he rose to his feet and made his way towards them, that he had been determined not to leave without speaking to Antonia once more.

Catching sight of him, her heart leaped. She stiffened and slipped her hand into Leo's arm in an instinctive gesture that was part-pride, part-defiance, part-protection. He looked down at her, smiling, confident ... and saw her apprehensive expression. He followed the direction of her gaze and frowned slightly.

Guy approached them with a sardonic smile touching his lips ... and although the smile lingered his eyes narrowed abruptly and fiercely as he noticed the diamond that flashed on her finger with that swift movement. He met her eyes and read the fierce challenge in their depths ... and he moved his shoulders in a slight, almost imperceptible shrug of indifference born of pride and dismayed defeat.

'I thought you left with Ames,' she said carelessly.

'It has been raining heavily ... I decided to

wait until the worst was over,' he explained smoothly.

Wounded to the very depths of her being by his indifference, she said brightly: 'How fortunate! It means that you can be the first to hear our news ... Leo and I are engaged!'

He nodded, his eyes inscrutable. 'You cannot surprise me, I'm afraid ... I knew it was inevitable,' he said—and his tone held a reminder that brought the colour into her cheeks. He turned to the man by her side and held out his hand. 'I must congratulate you, Bryce ... but I really feel that I should sympathise with you. For you can't know what marriage with Antonia entails, you know. She will lead you a merry dance, I'm afraid,' he said pleasantly.

Leo laughed, shaking hands with him, relieved to discover that Carlow did not mean to be difficult. 'I think you are wrong,' he said quietly, confidently ... and then his hand closed firmly and possessively over the slender fingers that rested on his arm. Antonia looked up at him swiftly, gratefully ... and Guy was shaken by the wealth of seeming affection in her beautiful eyes...

CHAPTER EIGHT

But there was no hint of his feelings in voice or expression as he said lightly: 'We must have a drink to celebrate the news.'

Leo glanced at his watch. 'I wish it were possible,' he said ruefully. 'But I'm due at the theatre for rehearsal ... we open next week, you know. May I take you up on that offer another time, Carlow?'

'Certainly ... we shall need to discuss Antonia's financial affairs, in any case. She has told you that I am her trustee, I suppose,' he said carelessly.

'I've heard something about it,' Leo said. He turned to the silent Antonia. 'Darling, I must go ... I'm late as it is. Why don't you join Guy in a drink ... I'll telephone you as soon as I'm free.' Briefly he raised her hand to his lips, oblivious to the dismay and annoyance that touched her eyes at his suggestion. He nodded to Guy and turned away with a feeling of relief that Antonia need not feel herself abruptly deserted while she had Carlow for company.

Antonia looked after him with a hint of panic in her thoughts. She had known about the rehearsal, of course ... had been quite resigned to parting with him so abruptly. But she had not bargained for being virtually

93

thrust into Guy's company ... and she turned slowly and reluctantly to meet his dark and faintly mocking eyes.

'I'm surprised that Bryce should be guilty of such bad timing,' he drawled.

She stiffened. 'What do you mean?'

'He has only just asked you to marry him, I gather ... knowing that he was due at a rehearsal and would have to abandon you at a moment when most engaged couples would wish to be together,' he said lightly.

She looked at him coldly. 'I don't think he meant to ask me over lunch, as a matter of fact,' she said impulsively and misguidedly.

He smiled sardonically. 'I see ... you forced his hand a little, did you? It obviously wasn't necessary as he seems to have been prepared for your agreement,' he added with a deliberate glance at the ring on her hand.

'Of course I didn't force his hand!' she snapped furiously. 'It ... it just happened!'

'Very conveniently, as it turned out,' he drawled. 'Although you couldn't have known that I was still about, I admit.' He smiled down at her ... a smile that held no hint of warmth or amusement. 'You were very pleased to be able to flaunt that vulgar and ostentatious stone in my face, weren't you?'

Her hands clenched involuntarily. 'If this were not a public place ...' she said in a low, seething tone.

'You would slap my face again? I doubt it,

94

Antonia ... I doubt it very much,' he said grimly. 'But this is a public place ... you are very right to remind me. We cannot quarrel here, you know,' he added and took her arm in no gentle grip and urged her towards the swing doors of the exit.

'I've no wish to quarrel with you,' she said coldly, so angry that she was very willing to believe that she had been mistaken in supposing that she loved him.

'Well, I mean to quarrel with you over this stupid farce of an engagement,' he told her with equal coldness—and hailed a passing taxi that obediently swung towards the kerb.

Antonia sank back against the cool leather seat, seething at the unceremonious way in which he had marched her from the restaurant and bundled her into the taxi. She was quite sure that she hated him at that moment and she turned the ring on her finger with a feeling of thankfulness that she would soon be married to Leo and need never have any more dealings with Guy Carlow than were strictly necessary!

He spoke briefly to the cab driver and got in beside her, sitting down at a considerable distance from her, she noticed, as though he intended to emphasise the barrier which separated them. Again she touched the ring as though it were a talisman and, noticing the gesture, he looked at her with every appearance of dislike and contempt.

95

'Stupid little fool,' he said without venom. 'Do you suppose that you are punishing me by choosing to marry Bryce?'

'No ... I know that you would see me married to *Lucifer* with a glad heart!' she retorted fiercely.

He smiled faintly. 'You exaggerate a little, as usual.'

Disdaining to reply, she turned her head to stare at the wet pavements and the scurrying pedestrians. Of all the men in the world why had Leo chosen to thrust her into Guy's company? It was unbearably ironic!

Guy was silent, studying her averted profile, hurt and infuriated by her folly, trying not to believe that she might be in love with Bryce and desperately clinging to the conviction that she had promised to marry the man in a mood of defiance.

Antonia was very conscious of him ... and it was painful to have him so near and yet know that they were and always would be worlds apart. She could not look at him, knowing the dislike and the hostility that she would find in his dark eyes. They might be strangers, she thought miserably ... and bitterly regretted the years and the lost opportunities when she might have won his affection rather than his contempt. She loved him so much that she could scarcely endure the pain that engulfed her, the longing for the touch of his hand, one comforting smile, one flicker of affection and understanding in those steely eyes. If only she could turn to him, hold out her hand to him, tell him that she loved him and had only agreed to marry Leo because she was so desperately unhappy and lonely without his love and understanding and sympathy. But it was utterly impossible. It was not pride that checked the impulse but the devastating knowledge that he would neither believe nor welcome her words.

It was better to be angry with him, to resent his arrogance, his hostility, his unwarrantable intrusion into her personal life, to do all she could to impress upon him that she loved and wanted Leo and meant to marry him and did not give a snap of her fingers for his or anyone else's views in the matter!

'Where are we going?' she asked stiffly.

'To the flat. Evelyn won't be there so we can discuss this business without interruption,' he said quietly.

She glanced at him briefly, suspiciously. 'How do you know Evelyn's plans?'

'Because I spoke to her on the telephone this morning.'

'Then you knew where to find me?' she said, a little bitterly.

'No ... but I thought it very likely that Evelyn would know where you were staying,' he explained. 'Eva wanted to know when you were planning to come home.'

'Home,' she said quietly, bitterly. 'I have no home.'

'Very dramatic,' he said drily. 'And quite untrue.'

'Do you imagine that I've ever thought of your house as my home?' she returned fiercely.

'No ... you've always regarded it as a convenient but temporary resting-place,' he said carelessly. 'But you have always been welcome to consider it as your home ... the fault lies with you, Antonia.'

'As always,' she said bitterly.

'As always,' he agreed smoothly.

She turned away from him and they were both silent during the few minutes that remained of the journey. The taxi drew up outside the tall block of luxury flats where Evelyn Hurst lived ... and Guy stepped down and turned to offer his hand to Antonia. She ignored it ... and he shrugged and turned to pay the fare. Antonia walked into the foyer and made her way to the lift ... and he joined her as the doors slid open. He looked down at her set expression and said in a conversational tone: 'Does Bryce suspect that you are a shrew at heart, I wonder?'

She threw him a swift, venomous glance. 'I hate you,' she said quietly.

Guy chuckled. 'It's the truth you hate, my dear.'

He followed her from the lift and she took the flat key from her bag and inserted it in the lock. 'Must you come in?' she demanded. 'I shall probably throw something at your head!'

'It's a risk I'm prepared to take,' he assured her lightly.

The flat was spacious and comfortable and very untidy. Antonia thrust a few items of flimsy lingerie behind a cushion, gathered up the magazines that lay on the floor where they had fallen, removed empty coffee-cups from a table and emptied ashtrays ... not from any tidy impulse but merely a desire to be doing something to delay the inevitable tempest.

Guy stood by the open window, looking down at the park on the other side of the road. She moved about the room, ignoring him ... and he sensed that she was nervous and apprehensive and wishing him at the other end of the world. Suddenly his anger evaporated ... and he was conscious only of a cold despair.

It would do no good to quarrel with her, he thought in bitter resignation. She obviously meant to marry Bryce ... whatever her motives. She had always gone her own way, never listening to advice or argument ... and she would not care how much she distressed her mother or anyone else by her actions.

Guy knew it was not the thought of her marriage to Bryce that troubled him so much, although he deplored the man's reputation and the obvious unhappiness that was in store for her ... it was the thought of her marriage to any man but himself. As she would never agree to marry him on any terms it did not really matter very much that he had lost her to Bryce, he thought bitterly. Lost her! She had never been his to lose, he reminded himself.

'Do you want coffee?' she asked, brusque through nervousness.

He turned. 'No. I must go ... I've a lot of work to do on the new book, Antonia.' He moved towards the door.

She stared at him in surprise. 'But you wanted to talk to me ... .'

'I've changed my mind,' he said quietly. 'You may marry Bryce with my blessing.'

'Am I supposed to be grateful?' she flared, dismayed by his sudden decision to leave, hurt that he did not mean to make the slightest attempt to prevent her marriage to Leo.

'You don't know the meaning of the word,' he said with a faint smile.

As he turned away once more, she blurted impulsively: 'Guy! Don't you care?'

He paused with his hand on the door. 'Why should it matter to me what you do with your life?'

'Then why were you so angry?' she challenged swiftly.

'Disappointed, my dear,' he amended drily. 'I thought you had more sense ... and more pride.'

'Leo loves me,' she said defiantly.

'He has loved a great many women,' he reminded her coldly.

'I know,' she said quietly. 'But one can love more than once in a lifetime, Guy.' She looked down at her slim hands. 'You said yourself that there were many kinds of loving.'

'Did I?' he returned carelessly. 'I don't remember that we've ever discussed the subject.'

'It's never been a subject that interested you, certainly,' she retorted swiftly. 'You've never loved anyone ... you don't know what it's like to be in love!'

'And you do?' he asked, amused.

She clenched her hands against the pain which swept through her. 'Yes ... I know,' she said quietly, despairingly.

His eyes darkened but he said lightly: 'You need not sound so tragic, you know ... after all, you have what you wanted—Bryce's ring on your finger.'

Her chin tilted abruptly. Horrified, she realised how close she had come to betraying herself. 'Yes, of course ... you will come to the wedding, Guy?' she said brightly.

'Eva will need my support,' he told her coolly.

She stiffened. 'Anyone would suppose I was going to the gallows instead of the altar!' she exclaimed with a brittle little laugh.

'The registry office,' he amended coldly. 'Caxton Hall, I imagine?'

'Yes ... yes, I suppose so,' she agreed, a little stunned to realise that it had not occurred to her to think so far ahead. His words brought home the enormity of the step she intended to take ... and dismay touched her heart as she recalled that Leo had been married before ... not once but three times!

Could there really be any happiness for her with a man who had proved his inability to make a success of marriage? Could there really be any security in linking her life with such a man?

Did Leo love her at all ... or did he merely want her and took marriage so lightly that he was willing to enter into it again in order to achieve his desire to possess her? How long would he continue to want her ... and would she soon find herself married to a man who did not hesitate to humiliate her by his pursuit of other women?

She had reached out blindly ... and Leo had chanced to be within reach and willing to oblige her desire to escape the loneliness that engulfed her. But it was a mistake ... a terrible mistake, she thought in panic. She could not marry Leo—or any other man while she loved and wanted Guy so desperately.

Leo's ring weighed heavily on her hand ... and on her heart as she stared down at it, touching it with incredulity and horror invading her thoughts.

Guy's lip curled. 'That ring means a great deal to you, I gather. I hope it brings you happiness,' he said curtly ... and the door closed behind him with a faint snap of finality.

Antonia felt as though her heart was torn from her body and taken with him ... she said his name in an agony of longing but it was too late and if he could have heard that betrayal of her love for him it would have meant nothing to him!

She wrenched Leo's ring from her finger and threw it across the room on a surge of revulsion. Then she buried her face in her hands and cried with all the pain and despair and fear of a lost child ... knowing that she *was* lost, would always be lost if she could not reach the sanctuary of Guy's love and need for her...

Guy walked briskly along the wet pavements, impervious to the rain on his bare head, blind and deaf to his surroundings ... torn and tormented by a jealousy that was shocking in its intensity, consumed by a sense of loss that made him feel that nothing in all the world could ever mean anything to him unless he owned the woman he loved so deeply, so desperately.

She was in love with Bryce ... very much in love ... so much in love that she meant to marry him although she might live in constant dread of losing him to any woman who chanced to catch his fickle attention. She did not care that the man made a hobby of marriage and was incapable of loving any of the women he married. She had surrendered her pride, her self-respect ... and Guy wished it were possible to despise her but he could only feel a reluctant compassion for he knew what it was to love, to be grateful for the smallest crumb of affection, to feel that anything could be sacrificed in the pursuit of happiness.

He could have borne her marriage to anyone but Bryce who must inevitably fail to make her happy, to be faithful to her, to protect her from hurt and humiliation. If she had loved any other man, he could have endured the knowledge and wished her happy with utter sincerity ... for her happiness must always be of prior importance to him. But he knew, as well as she must what was in store for her if she married Bryce ... and his heart ached that she was so ready to snatch at a brief and precarious happiness.

There was nothing he could do, he

thought despairingly ... but watch and wait and be there when she needed someone to turn to, someone to comfort her, someone to restore her confidence and give her fresh hope for the future.

He loved her so much ... and he was helpless. It was a bitter knowledge for the man who would sacrifice his life for her if it was demanded of him...

CHAPTER NINE

Eva's gentle blue eyes widened with dismay at the announcement. 'Engaged!' she repeated unhappily. 'Are you sure?'

Guy smiled wryly. 'You would not doubt it if you could see her pride and pleasure in the ring that Bryce has given her, Eva. An enormous knuckleduster of a diamond!'

She sighed. 'When do they mean to be married?'

'I didn't ask,' he said, almost curtly. 'Very soon, I imagine.' His mouth hardened. 'I wouldn't have been surprised to learn that she was already married.'

'But you assured me that she would never marry Bryce,' Eva reminded him, a little reproachfully.

'I didn't know then that she was in love with him,' he returned ruefully. 'There have been so many men in Antonia's life, after all ... and any one of them would have been a more acceptable choice,' he added bitterly.

Eva's slight shoulders lifted in a shrug of hopelessness. 'Oh, if she loves him...'

'You need not doubt that,' he said swiftly, reassuringly. 'She is very much in love—and very happy. Perhaps Bryce is right for her—how can we judge, Eva? Perhaps they are right for each other.'

'It doesn't seem very likely,' she said doubtfully. 'He isn't a very nice man, Guy.'

'But Antonia is never interested in "nice" men,' he reminded her drily. 'Bryce is the type she has always admired ... and it was inevitable that she should fall in love with a man of his calibre.'

'When is she coming home?' Eva asked anxiously.

He shook his head. 'This is not her home,' he said grimly. 'Or so she chose to inform me.'

'Oh, Guy!' she exclaimed. 'How could she say such a thing to you ... when you have always been so good, so kind, so generous!' She sighed again. 'I don't understand my own daughter ... I never did.' She placed a tentative hand on his arm. 'You are upset, Guy,' she said gently. 'I'm sorry ...'

Meeting her eyes, so filled with warm compassion and understanding, he knew a slight shock—and wondered how long she had known of his love for Antonia.

He did not attempt to dissemble. He smiled, a rueful look in his dark eyes. 'Yes . . . it's hard for me to accept, Eva.'

She felt suddenly impatient with him . . . an impatience born of disappointment and her dismay at Antonia's decision to marry Leo Bryce. 'She would have loved you if you had allowed her to do so,' she said . . . and the words were a reproach. Her eyes were troubled and her mouth was slightly tremulous. 'She was very fond of you at one time, Guy.'

He walked away from her, thrusting his hands deep into his pockets to hide their involuntary clenching. 'She was seventeen . . . a mere child,' he said quietly. 'Any responsible man would have done exactly what I did, Eva . . . one doesn't take advantage of a seventeen year old girl's emotions, you know.'

'It's a long time since she was seventeen . . . and I've thought on many occasions that she offered you an encouragement that you chose to ignore.'

He laughed . . . it was a grim, bitter little sound. 'I didn't choose to be added to her list of conquests, if that's what you mean! Every man has his pride, you know . . . and I was damned if I'd obey the lift of her finger merely to satisfy her ego!'

'Pride . . .' she mused. 'I've often

wondered how much in love a man has to be before he ceases to consider his pride. Women are not so foolish, thank goodness. Forgive me if I offend you, Guy ... but aren't you allowing pride to stand in your way even now? Does Antonia know that you love her? Perhaps she wouldn't want to marry Leo Bryce if she knew that she could be *your* wife!'

'My dear Eva!' he exclaimed impatiently. 'Can you really suppose that it would make any difference? She is head over heels in love with the man and determined to marry him.' He smiled at her warmly, indulgently. 'You are an incurable optimist—and a born romantic, I'm afraid. I'm sorry, Eva. There's nothing I can say or do to alter matters.'

'And you won't even try,' she said reproachfully.

'No ... I shall cling to my pride at all costs,' he said lightly.

'Cold comfort that will be when Antonia is married to that man!' she said crossly.

He went to her side and dropped a light kiss on her hair. 'Loving Antonia has never been a comfortable business,' he said simply. 'I have always hoped too much, you see ... but once she *is* married there can be no hope and one can learn to live with that knowledge. It's the constant hoping and the constant disappointment that has made it all so unbearable.'

She reached impulsively for his hand. 'I'm so sorry ... I didn't mean to be cross, Guy. But it's a great disappointment to me, too.' She smiled up at him penitently.

'But Antonia and I have never been together for five minutes without quarrelling,' he said in surprise.

'I know ... and that's exactly what made me so hopeful,' she said.

He frowned at the cryptic words. 'I don't understand,' he said slowly.

'No one could suppose that you were indifferent to each other,' she explained, smiling.

Guy laughed. 'Of course not ... we have always cordially disliked each other. I've loved your daughter for years, my dear ... but it would have been a great pleasure on many occasions to wring her neck, you know!'

'You should have made the attempt instead of walking from the room,' she said swiftly.

'Perhaps ... but it would have ended very differently and I should have been utterly lost,' he told her lightly.

She nodded in understanding. 'I suppose so ... and if you were so determined not to let her know how you felt ...' She did not finish the sentence.

'I wouldn't grant her the satisfaction of such a revenge—she would have found it very sweet, I assure you. She has never forgiven me for that episode when she was seventeen ... and I can't really blame her for I handled the whole thing very badly,' he said ruefully. He moved towards the door. 'I must change my clothes ... I walked too long in the rain.' A movement caught his eye and he glanced through the window. 'The Commander ... were you expecting him?'

'Oh yes ... he is taking me to the theatre,' she explained, swift colour touching her face to prettiness.

Guy smiled with a hint of mischief in his eyes. 'Now that's a thoroughly nice man who meets with my complete approval,' he said warmly. 'I shall be better pleased to hear of *your* engagement, Eva ... must I wait much longer, do you suppose?'

'Oh, hush! He will hear you!' she exclaimed, laughing softly. She looked at him a little doubtfully. 'Do you really think he would like to marry me, Guy?'

'I'm sure of it,' he said firmly. 'Does that please you?'

'Oh yes,' she said, blushing as deeply as a young girl. 'I must say I should like to marry Arthur ... he's such a dear and I believe I could make him happy.'

'I know you could,' he assured her ... and he moved towards her impulsively and kissed her cheek with a sudden surge of affection. 'If only your daughter was more like you,' he said ruefully.

'Would you have loved her so much?' she asked shrewdly. 'She has so much spirit ... and it is that which appeals to you, Guy.'

'You may be right,' he said carelessly ... and turned with a smile of greeting for the Commander as Sally ushered him into the room ...

He left them within a few minutes and the Commander set down his glass and turned to Eva, saying quite firmly: 'Has that young man been upsetting you, my dear?'

Eva raised startled eyes. 'Guy? No, Arthur ... not at all.' She smiled a little tremulously. 'Why do you ask?'

'You are not yourself,' he said bluntly. 'You don't deceive me, you know ... my eyes and ears are very sharp.'

She held out her hand to him. 'It isn't Guy, Arthur. He merely brought me some distressing news from town ... Antonia is going to marry Leo Bryce.'

He frowned. 'Just as you feared,' he said heavily. 'I'm sorry, my dear.' He took her hand and patted it gently. 'But it's better news than you expected, isn't it,' he said shrewdly. 'At least the fellow means to marry her.'

She hesitated. Then she said slowly: 'It must seem very unnatural of me ... but I can't help thinking that I should prefer *that* to marriage. He isn't *right* for her, Arthur ...

and it will be too late by the time she realises it.'

'You may be mistaken,' he said soothingly. 'But if the fellow is wrong for Antonia ... well, young people these days think nothing of divorce, you know. It doesn't seem to carry any stigma nowadays.'

'It is still a shocking humiliation ... and she is so young. How can she be so foolish? He has had three wives already, Arthur!'

'It seems very bad,' he agreed soberly. 'But she is over twenty-one and I suppose there is nothing you can do about it. She ... er ... wouldn't listen to you, Eva?'

She shook her head ruefully. 'She never listens to anyone,' she sighed. 'I shall try to talk to her, of course ... if I am allowed the opportunity. But it seems she has no intention of coming home ... and means to be married as soon as possible.' She rose to her feet, forcing a smile. 'But I mustn't burden you with my troubles, Arthur—and we don't want to be late for the theatre. I'll be ready in a few moments.'

He rose too ... and she paused, looking up at him with a faint question in her eyes. Her heart began to beat a little faster ... and she gave him a sweet, warm smile of encouragement.

He cleared his throat a little self-consciously—Eva waited, a hint of shyness in her smile.

But he merely said: 'Perhaps you would rather not go to the theatre tonight, after all?'

'But I'm looking forward to it,' she said eagerly. 'I won't allow Antonia to spoil our evening, the foolish child! After all, she isn't married to that man yet ... and who knows what might happen!'

He looked after her with tender affection in his gaze, touched as always by the perennial youth of her warm personality and the sweetness of her nature. She was much too good to be wasted on an old, retired naval man, he thought wryly ... and decided it was just as well that he had lost courage at the last moment. She was a woman with a very kind heart and he felt that she might have been a little lonely since her husband died or she might not have welcomed his awkward, inexperienced attentions with so much warmth and encouragement. But he must not suppose that her good-natured acceptance of him as a friend and admirer indicated a readiness to think of marrying again, he reminded himself cautiously.

He took out his handkerchief and blew his nose violently. He was becoming a sentimental old fool, he told himself sternly. He had spent nearly sixty years of his life without a woman by his side and it would not be such a great hardship to finish his span as a bachelor...

Eva hesitated on the threshold of the

room, a fur cape about her shoulders and a ridiculous little hat perched on her softly curling hair. Her tender heart swelled with affection and compassion as she watched that brisk business with the handkerchief and knew his thoughts as swiftly and surely as if he had spoken them aloud.

She moved towards him and he turned, a little startled, smiling almost self-consciously ... like a foolish boy, she thought tenderly.

'Dear Arthur ...' she said softly, holding out her hands to him.

He took them awkwardly—and laughed a little at his own clumsiness. 'I'm a clumsy old fool,' he said wryly.

She shook her head. 'I don't think you're any of those things.'

'You're very sweet, Eva ... I'm more grateful than I can say for all your kindness to me.'

'It isn't just kindness, Arthur ... and I don't want gratitude,' she told him firmly. She laughed youthfully as a startled look came into his eyes. 'Oh, Arthur!' she exclaimed in mock reproach. 'Do you mean to force me to throw myself at your head? Let me keep a little of my pride, my dear!'

His arms slipped about her ... perhaps a little clumsily but with reassuring firmness. She nestled against him as though she belonged in his arms ... as she did, in her own unshakeable opinion.

'Is it very foolish for a man of my age to tell you that he's in love?' he whispered against her hair.

'I shall be very disappointed if you say that you aren't,' she retorted lightly ... and raised her face to be kissed...

Guy was surprised and amused when he walked into the room some time later to find them sitting on the settee, hand in hand like young lovers. A sudden, almost guilty silence descended on the room.

'I thought you were going to the theatre,' he said, smiling.

Blushing, Eva rose to her feet. 'We changed our plans ... and made some new ones,' she said airily, moving to the decanters. 'Do you want a drink, Guy?'

He looked from her radiant, flushed face to the Commander who struggled to his feet, looking for all the world like a guilty schoolboy. He grinned sheepishly as he met Guy's dancing eyes.

'Certainly,' Guy said promptly. 'If I may drink a toast to your future happiness?'

Slightly taken aback, Eva glanced instinctively and with some uncertainty at the Commander. 'Well ... I'm not sure ...' she faltered, shyly hesitant.

The Commander was swift to perceive their dilemma. 'Eva means that I haven't actually proposed and she hasn't actually accepted,' he told Guy, his eyes twinkling.

'But I think you can safely drink that toast ... there isn't any doubt in *my* mind that we shall be married, right and tight.' Taking Eva's hand in his own, he tucked it firmly and possessively beneath his arm. 'Is there any doubt in your mind, my dear?' he asked tenderly.

She smiled up at him happily. 'None at all, Arthur,' she said gaily.

'I'm delighted to hear it,' Guy told them both with warm sincerity. He shook hands with the Commander and kissed Eva's cheek, wryly recalling his very different feelings at the announcement of that other engagement earlier in the day.

He went back to his study and his typewriter, leaving them to the eager, confident plans for the future ... but he was as incapable of working on his book then as earlier. He stared down at the blank sheet of paper in the typewriter—and turned away, wishing it were possible to escape into the more satisfactory world of fiction and forget for a few hours the difficulties and anxieties which beset him.

Eva would marry her Commander ... and he did not doubt their mutual happiness. Antonia would marry Bryce ... and be completely lost to him—and he wished he could find as much pleasure in the one thought as in the other.

They had shared his home for three years

and he would naturally miss them both. Eva's presence had been constant and they had lived together in perfect amity and understanding ... but he would not miss her so much as he would miss Antonia who had been away so much during those three years. Eva would not be far away, obviously ... they talked of buying a small house in the neighbourhood and no doubt he would see much of them in the future. He did not really suppose that Antonia would cut him completely out of her life but there would be an ever-widening gulf between them, he thought wryly. The easy intimacy of the past was gone for ever ... and he did not expect her to think of him with any degree of liking or interest in the future.

Yet it seemed incredible that she would no longer be an active, vital part of his life ... and the future seemed bleak and empty as he thought of all that he had lost, all he might have known if Antonia could only have loved him as he loved her...

Perhaps Eva was right and he had been wrong, he thought heavily ... perhaps he should have allowed Antonia to know all these years that he loved and wanted her, valued her more than anything else in the world. Perhaps she might have learned to love him if he had not suffered his pride to rule his heart. But he could not go so far as to imagine that Eva could be right in her eager, optimistic suggestion that Antonia might wish to marry him if she knew of his love. She was so obviously in love with Bryce, he thought bleakly, despairingly...

CHAPTER TEN

With a great deal of reluctance, Antonia retrieved the diamond ring from the floor and returned it to her finger.

She might have a great many faults but breaking her word was not among them, she thought bitterly ... she had promised to marry Leo and she would have to go through with it, and she supposed it really did not matter very much if she married him or any other man in the circumstances. Deep and lasting happiness with the man she loved was obviously no part of her destiny. Leo loved her and perhaps she could find a measure of contentment in being his wife—and perhaps she could contrive to content him more than any of his previous wives. She did not know the details of his marriages and divorces ... and she really did not wish to know. Let sleeping dogs lie, she thought wearily. Perhaps she could look upon this marriage as a challenge ... and prove to the world that the woman did exist who could evoke a lasting and loyal emotion in a man with

118

Leo's reputation.

She did not fear the publicity and the gossip that would attach to their engagement ... she had always enjoyed being the centre of attention and was too used to press interest in her affairs to dislike or resent it. On the contrary, she found herself hoping, a little foolishly, that Guy would meet with their linked names every time he picked up a newspaper in the coming weeks ... and realise how much he had lost by his indifference!

But she had determined not to dwell on thoughts of Guy and the might-have-been. The sooner she ceased to love him and need him and yearn for him the better, she thought bitterly ... and wondered how other people managed to fall in love on the rebound. It would be very convenient if she could will herself to love Leo instead of Guy ... and perhaps time and all the intimacy of marriage would effect such a change of heart.

Soon she would be married to Leo ... and he must never suspect that she did not love him. It was not going to be easy to play the part of loving and eager bride but at least she was not wholly indifferent to Leo. She had grown quite fond of him during the past week, spending so much time in his company and relaxing her defensive attitude where he was concerned and viewing him in a much warmer and more tolerant light than previously. She had been pleasantly surprised to find that he was not the thoughtless, irresponsible rake that she had supposed him to be ... he had behaved towards her with admirable restraint and a quiet, heart-warming tenderness that made it easy for her to believe that he really was in love with her. It had been a comforting thought, a balm for her hurt pride and aching heart ... and perhaps there had been an odd, foolish desire for revenge in her warm encouragement although she was well aware that Guy could not be hurt by anything she did. It was only human to hope that he would live to regret her marriage to another man although she knew it was a vain hope for he had never betrayed the least interest in her as a woman...

The engagement was celebrated that evening with a party of friends ... and it was the early hours of the morning before Antonia slipped between the sheets to snatch a few hours of sleep, feeling that she was irrevocably committed to marrying Leo. He was so happy, so proud ... and so much in love, she thought numbly. She ought to be thankful for his love and confident that he would do all he could to ensure her happiness ... but she did not feel anything any more.

No longer capable of pain or bitterness,

her heart seemed to be a dead thing hanging heavily in her breast ... and perhaps that was the only way she could face the future as Leo's wife. She had known too much agony of longing and futile loving in the past days ... no man could be worth so much pain and despair. She had not known that love could take such a toll of one's emotions ... and she felt that she would rather not be in love with anyone than experience such hell. She did not want to go on loving Guy ... and she welcomed the numbness of her heart. She could play her part as Leo's wife as long as she continued to be incapable of emotion and perhaps he need never know that he was married to a woman whose heart had died within her. He asked so little of her, she thought gratefully ... and wondered without interest if he knew that she did not love him at all and did not care because he wanted her on any terms. Some people were capable of such selfless love, she supposed ... the kind of love that gave without demanding anything in return. Perhaps that was the only true loving ... and if so she did not really love Guy at all. For if she were to allow herself to feel again she would want his love and need to be necessary to him as desperately as before and know that she could not face the future without knowing herself to be loved in return...

Every newspaper carried the story of their

engagement the following morning ... and Antonia glanced through them indifferently, neither amused nor annoyed by the uncompromising recital of Leo's past marriages and the blatant speculation as to the future success of his fourth venture into matrimony. She merely shrugged and pointed out how unimportant it all was to them, that they were confident about the future, when Leo blasted the reporters in no uncertain terms.

He had brought her flowers and a diamond bracelet that she allowed him to snap about her slender wrist without protest. He also brought her the news that his agent was delighted by their engagement and considered it excellent publicity for the new play.

'Dan suggested that we should get married on Thursday ... the day of the opening,' he said, a little diffidently.

Alarm flickered briefly in her lovely eyes but she had schooled her expression by the time he had finished lighting his cigarette and glanced at her. 'Is that what you want, Leo?' she asked quietly.

He raised her hand to his lips. 'I'd like to marry you today,' he said simply. 'But I mustn't rush you, my darling ... and it wouldn't be fair to marry you at a time when the theatre will be making so many demands on me. For your sake, we should wait a few weeks. I don't want you to regret anything, Antonia.'

He did not know how much she already had to regret, she thought wryly. There was no point in postponing their marriage. She would have to go through with it eventually and in her present frame of mind it did not really matter when the ceremony took place ... this week, next week, sometime—and preferably never, she thought bleakly!

She shrank from the thought of marrying him at all ... but she only had herself to blame and it was impossible to retract now. She had encouraged his attentions for months because she found it gratifying and flattering that she had succeeded in attracting and holding his interest, because she had enjoyed the envy of other women, the resentment of her other admirers, the disapproval of the world. She had deliberately led him into a proposal of marriage and she neither knew for certain nor cared particularly if he had always meant to ask her to marry him. She had made use of him without a qualm, seizing the comfort and reassurance and security he seemed to offer ... and it was too late to decide that she no longer needed that comfort and reassurance or felt that marriage to Leo would provide her with the security she sought.

She would not gain anything by changing

her mind, after all. If she did not marry Leo she would either live out her life in loneliness and longing for a man who did not want her or marry some other man who meant just as little to her ... so it might just as well be Leo that she married.

'I agree with Dan,' she said lightly. 'Next Thursday shall be our wedding day, darling.' She smiled at him. 'Why shouldn't we make good use of the publicity ... I want your play to be a hit!'

'And you doubt if it will make it on its own merits,' he said with a rueful laugh.

'No ... I don't mean that and you know it,' she said lightly. 'An actor of your standing doesn't need the boost of that kind of publicity ... but it won't do you or the play any harm, after all.'

'Being married to you will give me and the play an excellent boost,' he said softly, meaningly ... and drew her into his arms.

Antonia did not know whether to be thankful or dismayed that his skilful lovemaking could evoke some degree of response, albeit physical. She ought to be thankful, she supposed, for soon he would be demanding much more of her than her kisses. She would need every ounce of her resolution to surrender herself so completely to a man she did not love, to crush the thought of Guy at such moments, to avoid the mental deception that it was Guy's arms that held her, Guy's lips on her own, Guy's passion seeking and creating a response in her own being...

It was a busy day for the telephone never ceased to ring and it seemed that everyone she knew or had ever known found time to call at the flat to congratulate and exclaim and shower them both with questions. The news that they had decided on a date for the wedding reached the ears of the press by some mysterious means and a host of reporters soon descended on the flat.

There was little time for her to think or to feel anything but a detached admiration for the Antonia who claimed convincingly that she was very happy, very much in love, looking forward to being married and full of confidence in the future.

But she had a very strange conviction that the real Antonia was looking on in bewilderment and perplexity ... watching and listening while that other Antonia laughed and talked excitedly and appeared flushed and radiant and confident. And the real Antonia longed to declare that the whole thing was a mistake, just a publicity stunt, that she had no intention of marrying Leo Bryce or any other man. But she was silent because it was too late to retract and no one would listen to her, anyway.

No one was interested in the truth, she thought bitterly. No one really cared whether or not she loved Leo or wanted to marry him or would find any happiness as his wife. He was a star of stage and screen, a celebrity, a famous and wealthy actor with a public who delighted to deplore his marriages, his many affairs, and forgave him everything because he was a celebrity and a law unto himself. Everyone appeared to think that she was very clever and something out of the ordinary to coax Leo into marriage for the fourth time ... and she doubted if anyone imagined for a moment that she loved him!

Surrounded by a crowd of people, friends, virtual strangers, reporters, she clung to Leo like a drowning woman and plunged ever deeper into the morass with every word, every smile, every kiss bestowed on him for the benefit of the photographers.

She did not hear the telephone when it rang yet again. She turned when Evelyn touched her shoulder.

'Telephone ... it's Guy Carlow,' Evelyn said carelessly. 'Will you speak to him or shall I tell him that you haven't a moment right now?'

The name was a shock. She had not expected him to call her and she could not imagine why he had chosen to do so. He could not have anything to say that she had not already heard from him ... and there was nothing he could say which would change things now, she thought hopelessly.

126

She met Leo's eyes and realised the faint, suspicious apprehension in their depths. All unconsciously, she had tightened her hold on his hand as though the telephone call was a threat.

She smiled at him in swift reassurance and said over her shoulder to Evelyn, struggling for a carelessness to match her friend's: 'Oh, I'll speak to him ... I want to talk to my mother, anyway.'

'Take it on the extension,' Evelyn suggested sensibly. 'You won't hear a thing with all this hubbub.'

Antonia nodded ... and within a few moments she managed to escape into the bedroom. She stood with her back against the closed door for a moment, trying to marshal her thoughts, trying to control the violent thudding of a heart that she had supposed to be stilled for ever.

Slowly she moved to the telephone and picked up the receiver. Her hands were trembling and she felt sick and cold and foolishly weak with the fierce, strange excitement that sprang from the very core of her being as she anticipated the sound of his voice.

She pulled herself together, knowing she dare not betray that surge of emotion. 'Hallo, Guy,' she said brightly, coolly. 'Sorry to keep you waiting but it's bedlam here ... we are besieged by the press and half the world has come to congratulate us, it...'

He broke into her words abruptly. 'Will you come home, Antonia? It's Eva ... a heart attack. She's very ill, I'm afraid.'

Stunned, shaken, incredulous, she caught her breath on a little gasp. 'Oh no! Guy, it isn't possible...'

'It has to be!' he said curtly ... and she had never known his voice to sound quite so cold, so harsh.

'Oh, of course I'll come ... I didn't mean that,' she hastened to explain. 'It's just—I didn't know that Eva was having trouble with her heart!'

'It was a shock to me, too,' he said grimly. 'Apparently she has known about it for some months and hasn't mentioned it to either of us. How soon can you be here?'

'Is it ... so urgent?' she asked uncertainly, her heart leaping with dread.

He was silent for a moment. Then he said gently: 'She's very ill, Antonia...'

She could not mistake the tender regret of his tone nor the implication of the words. 'No ... oh no!' she exclaimed on a sob. With an effort she caught back the tears but they muffled her voice as she added: 'I'll come now, Guy ... straight away.'

He said quietly: 'Ask Bryce to bring you ... I don't want you at the wheel of a car with this on your mind.' He hesitated and then added gently: 'You may be glad of his

128

presence, you know.'

'No! I'll come alone!' she said in swift refutation but he had already rung off and she put down the receiver, frightened, sick with dismay and apprehension ... and yet at the very back of her mind, scarcely acknowledged, lurked the thought that if her mother died no one could expect her to marry Leo so soon...

It was difficult to persuade Leo that she did not need or want his company, that she was quite capable of driving the car ... and she knew that he was hurt by her persistent refusal, her stubborn independence, her impatient dismissal of his arguments. She appreciated that he felt it was his right to be with her and to comfort her if it proved necessary—but she knew that she could not endure his presence or his comfort at such a time.

The reporters melted away as soon as they heard of her sudden need to go home ... a little more publicity to attach to the engagement, she thought bitterly. It took longer to be rid of the friends who clamoured for details she lacked herself and almost overset her composure with their ready, superficial sympathy. Only Evelyn and Leo showed any understanding and they contrived a swift and easy departure for her ... and as she set off on frustratingly busy roads she thought wryly that if Leo had not been so insistent that she needed him she might have been on her way half an hour before! She had left him with Evelyn and found herself wishing wholeheartedly that they might discover a mutual attraction before she returned to London and solve one at least of her problems!

The miles she had covered so many times without a second thought now seemed to be endless. The hills had never been so steep or the lanes so treacherous in their sudden curves and she fumed at every hazard that forced her to slacken speed.

It was a lovely day but she had no appreciation for the verdant beauty of the fields and trees and hills bathed in bright, warm sunshine. For she did not know what news would be waiting for her at Mersleigh End and she was consumed with fear. Every thought and feeling was driven from mind and heart except for the love she knew for her mother and the regret she suffered for the many times she had failed to show that love, the many times she had been impatient and rude and contemptuous, how many times she must have hurt and disappointed the gentle, kindly, sweet-natured woman that she had never valued sufficiently until she was so near to losing her for ever...

CHAPTER ELEVEN

As the car turned into the drive and screeched to a halt, Guy walked out into the bright sunshine and went to meet Antonia.

She scrambled from the car and ran towards him, searching his face for news, good or bad. He sent her a swift nod of reassurance ... and she was flooded with a fierce relief that made her suddenly weaken at the knees.

She stumbled and instinctively he caught her ... for the briefest of moments his arms were about her and then he released her. Antonia looked up at him, her heart hammering ... but she was not thinking of Guy or her love for him in that moment. She had scarcely been conscious of his strong arms supporting her, his nearness or the swift concern which had flown to his dark eyes.

'I'm all right,' she said impatiently, her anxious eyes turning immediately to the house. 'How is she?'

'Murray is with her and she seems to be responding to treatment,' he said reassuringly. 'It was touch and go when I telephoned, though ... I admit I anticipated the worst.'

'And now?'

'Murray seems to think she will be all right although she will have to take great care of herself in future,' he explained. He looked down at her white face, noting the strain in her eyes, the fierce effort to control the tremor of her lips. 'You've been very anxious,' he said gently. 'I'm sorry you were frightened, Antonia ... but so was I. It was unfortunate that I had to call you away from town at this particular time ... it must be very inconvenient.'

Suspecting a sneer, anger raced through her ... the inevitable reaction to the relief which had brought her close to fainting for the first time in her life. 'Oh, don't be so stupid!' she flared. 'You must hold me in contempt if you imagine I wouldn't fly home when my mother is ill and needs me! Convenience doesn't enter into it!' She stalked past him towards the house, seething, too angry to be hurt although pain would seep into her heart later, she knew.

Guy hurried after her and caught her arm. 'You need a drink,' he said quietly. 'It's been a shock ... and I told you not to come alone, you know. Anything might have happened on the road!'

She jerked her arm away from his hand. 'Nothing did ... I don't need a keeper!'

He looked down at her, his eyes dark and inscrutable. 'You should have had someone with you,' he repeated firmly. 'I suppose

Bryce had a rehearsal!'

This time the sneer was unmistakable and she looked at him coldly. Leo meant very little to her but she would defend injustice against a stranger! 'I came alone because I wished to be alone ... anyone but you could understand my feelings at such a time. May I see my mother ... or are you delaying me for a reason?'

His lips compressed. But he reminded himself that she had driven thirty miles under considerable stress and she could be forgiven for losing her temper in such circumstances. 'I expect Murray will allow you to see her for a few minutes ... but you are much too agitated at the moment, Antonia. You need a drink and a cigarette and a few minutes to calm down ... or Eva will suppose herself to be at death's door. You look quite ghastly, my dear,' he said lightly.

She was swift to appreciate the logic of his words. 'Very well ... but I don't want a drink. Just leave me alone for a while, will you? I'll come in shortly.' She fumbled in her bag for cigarettes and lighter ... extracted a cigarette with shaking fingers and fought back the tears that brimmed on her lashes. She seemed to have lived through an eternity of highly-strung emotion in the past week ... and she had almost reached the end of her tether.

Guy stood irresolute and then, as she flashed him an angry, resentful glance, he turned on his heel and went into the house. There was nothing he could do or say, he thought wearily ... she wanted nothing from him, neither sympathy nor comfort nor support and certainly not the wealth of love he had to offer her. He had come close to betraying himself when he held her briefly in his arms ... but she had rebuffed him impatiently, resenting his touch as it was obvious that she resented his affection and concern for Eva.

It was typical that Antonia had ignored his advice and made the journey alone ... and it was equally like her to refuse Bryce his right to be with her at such a time. She was so proud, so wilful, so stubborn ... and yet she was loyal, he thought, recalling how swiftly she had bridled at his sneer against the man she was to marry. He admitted that the comment had been unworthy of him and regretted the moment it was uttered ... but he was human as any other man and not in the least immune to a very natural jealousy.

She had been so gay, so confident, so excited and triumphant, obviously revelling in the publicity attaching to her engagement, when she came to the telephone. Guy had spoken more abruptly than he had intended, consumed with anger and jealousy and bitter resentment that was all the sharper because of his anxiety for Eva. Unfairly, he had felt that Antonia should have sensed that all was not right at home ... unfairly, he had felt that she would have known if she had been at home as she should have been at a time when she was planning to be married. She was so thoughtless, so careless of everything but her own desires.

He did not find it impossible to find fault with her, simply because he loved her ... his love was born of long knowledge and association and understanding and was not newly sprung to life and blinded by the magic dust which led many a lover into the snare of illusion. He had no illusions about the lovely, spoiled, self-willed Antonia—but he loved her very deeply for all the faults which were not so much faults as symptoms of her immaturity.

It was some time before she came into the house. Murray was just leaving, having explained the situation to Guy and promised to send a trained nurse as soon as possible. Guy noticed that Antonia was very calm and composed for all her pallor and she questioned Murray in level tones and accepted his answers and reassurances with quiet understanding. Murray left and Antonia went to her mother's room and Guy ordered coffee to be served in the sitting-room. She joined him before Sally had arrived with the tray and he glanced up quickly, anxiously.

'She's asleep,' Antonia said quietly. 'I didn't disturb her.' She sank into a chair. 'She looks so ill ...' she blurted impulsively.

Guy nodded. 'She is ill,' he said gently.

'I don't understand how she could have kept it from us!' she exclaimed. 'All these months!'

'I know ... I blame myself, too,' he said quietly.

She looked at him steadily, a challenge in her eyes. 'I have been away so much—but you have been here. How *could* you fail to notice?' He winced slightly at the reproach in her voice and she said quickly, penitently: 'Oh, I'm sorry! I shouldn't have said that ... it wasn't fair!'

'But quite justified,' he returned. 'I should have noticed, of course ... I should have suspected the tablets that she claimed were for indigestion. But she has seemed so well, so happy ... I told you that there has been a marked change since she met the Commander.'

'I'm surprised he isn't haunting the house,' she said wearily. 'Or doesn't he know?'

'He was with her,' he said, a little curtly. 'It was a great shock to him and I persuaded him to go home and rest just before you arrived. There was nothing he could do ... and so much he wished he could do. Poor devil! He has taken it very much to heart and thinks he is entirely responsible, I'm afraid.'

'Why on earth should he?' Antonia demanded in surprise.

'Murray suggests that the excitement of making wedding plans was too much for her heart ... and I daresay he is right. She has been as excited as a girl,' he said ruefully.

Her eyes widened. 'Wedding plans? Eva and the Commander?'

'I'd forgotten that you couldn't know ... it happened last night,' he told her. His mouth took on a faintly sardonic curl. 'But I doubt if you are very interested in the excitement of your own plans. You dislike it very much, I know ... but you are as powerless to prevent it as Eva is to prevent your marriage so you may as well accept it with good grace.'

'But I don't dislike it,' she returned quietly, sincerely.

His eyes were sceptical. 'A sudden change of heart? I suppose you view everything through different eyes now that you are looking forward to your own marriage. When does that happy event take place, by the way ... or haven't you set a date?'

She reached for a cigarette to cover the swift anguish of her heart that he could take such a casual interest in her future. 'We decided on next Thursday ... to coincide with the opening of Leo's play,' she said, as carelessly as she could.

His jaw clenched and a tiny pulse hammered in his cheek. The natural impatience of a woman in love combined with innate impulsiveness should have prepared him for such haste to be married ... but he had not expected to relinquish her so inevitably so soon.

He rose abruptly, snapping his lighter into life and offering the flame to her cigarette ... needing to be doing something in that moment to conceal the tide of emotion that swept over him. Automatically she covered his hand with her own to steady the flame ... it was a trick she had acquired in her teens and always managed to imbue with a hint of warm, coquettish intimacy. He stiffened slightly at her touch ... and she looked up at him swiftly, startled. 'So soon,' he said lightly, smiling ... but his eyes were cold and untouched by the smile that quirked his lips. 'Bryce means to make sure of you before you follow another impulse and return his ring, I suppose?'

She stifled annoyance with an effort. It was always too easy to quarrel with Guy—and she had no heart to bandy words with him or for the continuation of their estrangement. She smiled a little tautly. 'Very likely,' she agreed lightly as though she responded to a humour that had not existed in the words. 'We didn't mean to be married so soon ... but there is nothing to wait for,

138

after all.' If she waited for the rest of her life she would wait in vain for him to make any effort to prevent her marriage to Leo, she thought hopelessly.

'I suppose not,' he said stonily. 'And now that Eva has obliged you by recovering you need not postpone your arrangements. But I expect that has already occurred to you.'

Indignation flared to life at the injustice of his mocking words. But she would not afford him the satisfaction of knowing that she had already decided that Leo must wait until her mother was well on the road to recovery. She did not wish to leave her too soon ... she might be needed ... anything might happen—and she would not admit even to herself that she hoped against hope that a way out of her promise to marry Leo might present itself during the next few weeks.

With a slightly tilted chin, she returned brusquely: 'Naturally it has ... it is only human to think of the personal angle in every crisis.'

Their eyes met and held for a moment ... and then Sally entered the room with the belated coffee tray. Guy thanked her absently and Antonia leaned forward to deal with the coffee pot. Sally had brought some clumsily-cut sandwiches but if they had been wafer-thin and appetisingly delectable Antonia could not have viewed them with anything but indifference.

As Guy accepted his cup from her hand, he said abruptly: 'You do realise that it won't be possible for Eva to attend your wedding ... it will be many weeks before she is well enough to contemplate her own.'

She shrugged. 'I didn't really expect either of you to attend, you know. You are very much against the whole idea, aren't you ... both of you?'

'Eva is naturally concerned for your happiness,' he said quietly. 'She feels that you are rushing into marriage with a man who has scarcely proved himself to be a considerate and loyal husband in the past.'

'Leopards do change their spots sometimes,' she said tartly.

He smiled sardonically. 'Do they?'

'If the incentive is great enough!'

'You must explain your theory to a zoologist one day,' he commented drily.

'It pleases you to mock ... but Leo loves me very much,' she retorted, on the defensive. 'I know he would never do anything to hurt me!'

Her loyalty, her faith in the man she meant to marry wounded him deeply ... it was such a waste of the generous warmth of heart that he had always known she must possess and had always hoped that only his love for her and her sweet, glad response would evoke. 'I expect his previous wives held the same belief,' he said sharply. 'But Bryce appears to be a man who would trample on anyone who stood in his way, utterly ruthless in the pursuit of his own desires. You have that much in common, I suppose ... and birds of a feather deal very well together!'

He struck at her, wanting to hurt as she had hurt him ... and he did not know how well he succeeded.

Her face flamed. 'You have a very poor opinion of me,' she said quietly, bitterly.

'I've known you for some years,' he returned smoothly.

'And you've never really known me at all!' she threw at him impatiently. 'You've always wanted to believe the worst of me ... you've never looked beyond the surface!'

'I don't go out of my way to invite disappointment, my dear,' he drawled cuttingly. 'You see, I should have been very pleased to learn that you are not as selfish and heartless, as irresponsible and as conceited as you appear to be!'

She had no defence. It was so true that she had been all of those things. It was an appalling indictment but it was completely justified. She had been selfish, considering nothing and no one but herself. She had been heartless, flirting recklessly with any man who came her way, encouraging admiration and affection and even love without caring that she offered nothing in return and hurt the men in her life by her indifference and careless rejection. She had been irresponsible in many ways ... and conceited enough to imagine that everyone must love and admire her, that she could do no wrong or else meet with generous forgiveness on all sides, that even Guy had found it impossible not to love her and, resenting her lack of interest in him, treated her with every appearance of dislike and contempt.

She had been such a fool ... such a silly, blind, careless fool. It was futile to suppose that things might have been very different if he had not hurt and humiliated her so much all those years ago. She would have behaved in exactly the same way, confident of retaining his affection and interest whatever she did ... and she would probably have tired of him very quickly, bored by his attentions and his demands as other men had always bored her, swiftly seeking fresh conquests.

But she was paying the penalty for her folly ... and would continue to do so for the rest of her life, she thought bleakly. For Guy did not love her in the least and she could marry Leo or any other man with his blessing ... and it would do no good to defend herself, to claim that she had changed, that she regretted the past and intended to be worthy of his liking and respect if nothing else in the future. He did not believe that a leopard *could* change its spots ... and if he were to discover that she loved him and would do anything to earn his approval he would merely feel that she had come by her just deserts! Surprised by her silence, by the complete absence of anger in her expression, he glanced at her curiously. It was not like Antonia to ignore such bait ... he had expected a furious outburst, would have welcomed it rather than the stricken look in her lovely eyes.

Deeply hurt, her heart feeling that it must break, she took refuge in the light touch ... for he must not know the devastating effect of his words. 'You never pull your punches, do you?' she accused with a little, choked laugh. 'Thank heavens Leo doesn't know me as well as you do ... or he would certainly not wish to marry me!' She rose to her feet, needing to escape before she betrayed the pain that engulfed her. 'I ought to telephone him, by the way,' she said lightly ... and went from the room, scarcely knowing how she had contrived to keep her composure. For if she had been so foolish as to hope ... and heaven knew she *had* hoped ... she realised at last the utter hopelessness of loving a man who despised her too much to conceal his contempt. She ought to hate him for such wanton, deliberate cruelty at a time when she particularly needed his kindness and understanding and compassion ... but she could only feel an agony of love and longing and bitter regret for all that she had done to incur that contempt...

CHAPTER TWELVE

It had been a severe attack and the memory of fear and shock still shadowed the blue eyes as Eva Standen lay back on her pillows and held out her hand to her beautiful daughter. She smiled courageously, reassuringly, anxious to erase the concern and fear that darkened Antonia's own eyes.

Antonia had entered the room with every intention of being brightly cheerful and gaily scolding her mother for giving everyone such a fright. But she was suddenly a frightened, insecure child in need of her mother as she approached the bed ... and she dropped to her knees beside the bed and laid her cheek on the slim hand that seemed so frail, so white and the scalding tears welled and spilled over without restraint.

She cried quietly while Eva gently stroked her bent head ... but it was only a few moments before she fought back the tide of unhappiness that had sought relief in those tears and raised a rueful face to her mother's gaze.

'I'm an idiot,' she said. 'I'm not supposed

to be crying all over you … Guy would be furious.'

Eva smiled at her tenderly. 'Darling, I'm very touched,' she said softly. 'It makes me very happy to know that you care so much.'

Impulsively Antonia kissed the slender hand. 'Of course I care! But how could you know when I've been such a beast to you at times, so selfish and mean and thoughtless. Forgive me!'

Eva's eyes were touched with faint sadness. 'Antonia … that is the last thing you ever need to say to me, you know,' she said quietly. She touched her daughter's cheek with gentle fingers and then said briskly: 'Do let me see your ring, darling … and I want to know all your plans. When is the wedding?'

Antonia rose and sat on the edge of the bed. Reluctantly she held out her left hand and smiled obediently as Eva exclaimed her admiration of the beautiful stone. 'The wedding?' she repeated airily. 'Oh, not for weeks … not until you are well again. I don't mean to be married unless you can be present to shed the inevitable tear and wish me happy, you know.'

Eva smiled … but her eyes were shrewd as she studied her daughter. 'And will you be happy?' she asked quietly. 'Is this what you really want, darling?'

'Yes, of course,' Antonia said, a little too

quickly, a little too emphatically. 'Leo is a dear ... I know you don't like him very much but you don't really know him very well. And, like most actors, he always plays to an audience ... but he's entirely different when we are alone. I expect we shall be very happy ... and confound all the optimists who are laying odds on how long this marriage will last!' Her laugh was slightly too gay, almost brittle ... and Eva gave an almost imperceptible little nod as though Antonia had confirmed a suspicion. 'But I want to know about *your* wedding plans,' Antonia went on with a hint of light reproach. 'How odd that we should both become engaged on the same day ... but I admit that your engagement was more predictable than mine,' she added teasingly.

Eva coloured slightly and her smile was shy. 'I don't know,' she demurred. 'Arthur is a very modest man ... he was really quite astonished to learn that I always meant to marry him.'

'I suspect that you gave him a little push,' Antonia teased, laughing.

'Oh, several pushes, darling!' Eva admitted lightly, mischief glinting in her blue eyes. Then she paused and added quietly, seriously: 'Men are such odd creatures, you know ... sometimes they just won't go after what they want for the strangest of reasons. Strange to a woman, anyway. Modesty in

146

Arthur's case ... pride in some cases—fear of being laughed at in others. It's so silly, isn't it? If only they realised that a woman is always touched and pleased to learn that she is loved ... even when she is quite unable to accept or return such depth of feeling. I've always thought that it's the men who love the most deeply who hesitate to admit their feelings ... who will even pretend complete indifference rather than be suspected of caring so much.'

Antonia digested the words in silence, a faint frown touching her eyes ... she had the oddest conviction that her mother was trying to convey something to her but the thought that leaped so instinctively to mind was rejected even before it could encourage hope to leap in her heart. Her mother was an incurable romantic: no doubt she had been disappointed and upset by her engagement to Leo and perhaps she was not wholly convinced that it was a marriage based on mutual love for Eva could be disconcertingly shrewd at times; perhaps she had always cherished a fond hope that Guy and her daughter might eventually settle their differences by falling in love ... for Antonia did not doubt that her mother had referred to Guy in those odd remarks.

Surely no one in their right mind could suppose that Guy cared anything for her ... and Eva must know even better than most that he viewed her with utter contempt and that his indifference owed nothing to pretence, Antonia thought bleakly ... and wished she could find some grain of comfort in her mother's words.

She wondered with a sudden stab of anxiety if Eva believed it was comfort she was offering ... and if her mother knew or suspected that she loved Guy. Then she reminded herself how impossible it was that Eva could know or suspect when she had known the truth such a little time herself and had not been at home to betray her inner turmoil of emotion. Eva could only be expounding a theory born of her own affair with the Commander ... and it was only her own stupid sensitivity that caused her to attach importance to a trivial speech.

She said lightly: 'It's an interesting theory and you are probably correct, darling. But I musn't tire you with so much talking ... I expect Guy is outside the door with a stopwatch for I promised not to stay longer than ten minutes.' She leaned forward to kiss her mother's cheek. 'Try to sleep—and have happy dreams about the future with your Arthur, darling,' she said tenderly ... and went quietly from the room.

Eva sank back on the pillows with a faint sigh. She had tried ... but Antonia either would not or could not understand. She wondered again about those tears ... as she had wondered when the bent head lay under her gentle hand and Antonia's slight body had shuddered with the unhappiness she could not suppress any longer. Eva had pretended that she believed the sobs to be a natural reaction ... inevitably Antonia had been upset and frightened to learn of that ridiculous heart attack ... but in her heart she had known that it was much more than relief and concern and anxiety and distress. Antonia was desperately unhappy ... for all her lightness of manner, the bright gaiety of her voice, the laughter and gentle teasing that had followed the tears there had been the shadow of persistent pain in her beautiful eyes and her lovely face had been a little too fine-drawn.

She was certainly not happy in that stupid engagement, Eva thought firmly ... and wondered at Guy's blindness, recalling that he had described Antonia's 'pride and pleasure' in the ring that she had shown to her mother with faint but unmistakable hesitation and an obvious reluctance to talk about her wedding plans.

Guided only by her instinct—which had not failed her where Guy was concerned—she felt strongly that the key to Antonia's unhappiness lay in her difficult relationship with Guy Carlow ... and Eva would not be at all surprised to learn that her daughter was very much in love with the man whose pride and obstinacy matched her own.

She sighed again ... for she had lived long enough to know that one could not interfere in these matters and that there was nothing she could do or say to break down the barrier which they had erected for themselves throughout the years. They must find their own way to each other ... and there was always a way if love was real and lasting and indestructible ...

Guy was not outside the door. As Antonia made her way to her own room she did not know whether to be relieved or disappointed ... she desperately wanted to be near to him but he was a cold, unfriendly stranger and she did not find it easy to talk to him without betraying that his attitude hurt her deeply.

She caught the faint sound of his typewriter and knew that she need not expect to see him again that evening. Once in her own room, she felt aimless and lonely ... there was nothing to do but glance idly through a book, listen to some music, smoke a cigarette or two and finally relax in a hot bath and go to bed. She was tired ... mentally and emotionally exhausted. Yet she did not believe that she would sleep for every sense was alerted by Guy's presence beneath the same roof. She had never been so aware of him ... and she had never found it so impossible to go to him and find a little balm for her heartache just in being with him, talking to him, in feeling that he wanted and welcomed her company. For all their quarrels of the past it had always been a simple matter to approach him again with a smile, a light and teasing approach, and to slip easily into the familiar intimacy of long association.

But this new barrier was not due to any quarrel ... although they had exchanged bitter words. If Guy had made allowances for her in the past he would not do so again ... he had virtually cut her out of his life and the knowledge filled her with a terrible and devastating sense of loss...

She saw little of him during the next few days, keeping out of his way as much as possible and knowing that he did not seek her company, dreading that an impulsive word or an instinctive reaction to a remark or an accidental touch or even his very presence in the same room might betray the secret that he must not learn...

Guy turned away from the open window abruptly, consumed by that fierce jealousy which frightened him a little with its intensity. He supposed it was very natural that Antonia should speed to meet the approaching car and should go into Bryce's arms so gladly ... after all, she was in love with the man and it was all of three days since she had seen him.

He was surprised that she had not gone

151

back to town and her friends and her fiancé as soon as it became obvious that Eva was making excellent progress. Antonia had not betrayed any impatience to return ... and Guy felt her attitude was strange in a prospective bride who must have many arrangements to make for her rapidly-approaching wedding. She had not even made a brief journey to town to see Bryce who had been too involved with last-minute rehearsals and activities for the new play to visit her.

It was all very odd ... but her warm welcome for Bryce dispelled any suspicion, any faint hopes he might have cherished, that the engagement was not as valid as it appeared. And he could not doubt her feeling for the man, Guy thought wryly ... they might have been separated for months instead of days!

He sat down at his desk and forced himself to concentrate on the work which was suffering through his mental and emotional turmoil. He knew that every word he had written in recent days would need to be revised or scrapped ... but it was occupation for his thoughts when he could briefly drive Antonia out of mind.

It was a warm, still day and Antonia sat with Leo on the terrace, striving for gaiety, for a seeming delight in his company ... completely unaware that her light tones, her musical laughter, her apparent happiness carried to Guy and caused his heart to twist with pain and bitter anger.

She had been glad to see Leo but the warm rush of feeling was no more than affection and gratitude ... and her pleasure was tempered by a sense of guilt that she could not respond to the eager ardour of his greeting. They had been in constant touch by telephone but such contact had made little demand on her emotions ... it was not so easy to suffer his arms about her and his lips on her own without instinctive rebellion and she had extricated herself as swiftly and as tactfully as she could. Yet there was a certain comfort in knowing that he had missed her, that she was loved and desired ... his tender, almost humble adoration was in such contrast to the hurtful indifference of Guy's attitude towards her. She felt she understood why a woman might choose to marry a man who loved her even though she did not love him ... it was so much less painful to be loved than to be the lover suffering all the delights and despairs, the hopes and heartaches, the reliefs and the anxieties of loving and longing.

Leo's perceptions were sharpened by the deep and lasting love he knew for her ... he had sensed the effort it was for her to endure his embrace and known immediate alarm. Sensitive to every cadence of her voice, every expression that flickered in her eyes, every taut nerve in her body, he knew without a shadow of doubt that she had deceived him and that whatever her motive in promising to marry him there was no love for him in her heart.

She was too tense, too anxious to convey an emotion that simply did not exist, too gay, too light of heart and too talkative ... and he felt that she was desperately seeking to avert any mention of their future. He responded as she wanted and obligingly did not bring up the subject ... but his heart was sore as he thought of the arrangements he had snatched the time to make and the confidence and happiness with which he had looked forward to making Antonia his wife.

He wondered if she still meant to marry him. It was not an unknown situation, after all—and he would take her on any terms with the hope that she would learn to love him in time. Love did not leave much room for pride ... and he wanted her too much to be noble or generous. If she would marry him without love then he had no desire to dissuade her.

He had been too ready to believe that she loved him, he thought wryly ... remembering that she had kept him at a distance for months and then abruptly offered a warmer, intriguing, provocative encouragement which had not failed to bring him to the point of proposing marriage if that was what she had intended. To some extent, she had virtually thrown herself at his head, he thought in restrospective surprise ... wondering that he had not suspected the strategy in a woman who had the reputation of being a puritan with an innate coquetry of manner that promised much and rewarded the hopeful with angry disappointment. He should have suspected that sudden change of heart ... but he had been too thankful to question her motives or her true feelings.

Later in the day, lunching with Antonia and Carlow, he was inevitably struck by their overdone courtesy towards each other and the lack of warmth or familiarity in their attitudes. They met and smiled and talked as strangers ... and although he knew that Antonia had never been able to charm the man who seemed to regard her with sardonic amusement and faint disapproval, it seemed to him that the cool and hostile indifference was new and slightly bewildering and a little disturbing.

Carlow was the perfect host ... courteous, amusing and pleasant—perhaps a little too pleasant, Leo thought shrewdly. It was an uncomfortable meal for he felt as though he had called on a married couple who had been interrupted in the middle of a bitter quarrel, were bound by convention to entertain him and to pretend that all was well between them—not very convincingly, at that—and were longing for his departure so that they could continue to hurl abuse at each other.

Antonia was careful not to meet Carlow's eyes, Leo noticed ... and Carlow allowed his gaze to rest on her a little longer than necessary with a hint of angry contempt in his dark eyes whenever she gave her attention to him.

It suddenly dawned on Leo with shattering conviction that they were lovers who had quarrelled and in a fit of pique she had taken the first man who showed willingness to marry her. It was odd that a woman could find any degree of satisfaction in such a revenge or could be so blind or indifferent to the pain that she inflicted not only on herself but the two men concerned in the business ... but it was not so rare as to seem impossible. He was astonished by his own readiness to be deceived, to be used to such ends ... but he loved her too much to surrender her to any man, he thought grimly.

She would never be happy with Carlow ... he was a man of moods, difficult, temperamental, autocratic and harsh—not at all suited to the lovely, sensitive Antonia. But *he* could and would make her happy ... and he was confident that she did not mean to extricate herself from their engagement. In his experience, women were utterly ruthless

156

when happiness was at stake and if Antonia had changed her mind she would not hesitate to admit it. It was very natural that she might know a few doubts ... but perhaps in her heart she felt that marrying him was a wise step and would lead to greater happiness than she thought possible at the moment.

He was determined not to offer her any loophole ... he meant to make her his own, come what may! And she would not have any cause to doubt his confidence or to suspect his knowledge, born of instinct alone though it might be, that she did not care for him as he had believed.

CHAPTER THIRTEEN

Antonia was shocked to discover that she was a coward. But she simply could not summon the courage to tell Leo that she did not love him and could not marry him although she despised herself for her weakness.

She had always been so insensitive to the feelings of others that it came as a shock to realise the compassion and fierce regret she felt for encouraging Leo to love her as he undoubtedly did. She shrank from hurting the man who believed implicity in her love and treated her with such tenderness, such gentle humility, such warm and appealing consideration. There were depths to Leo that no one had suspected ... least of all herself, she thought ruefully. He was the kind of man she should have been able to love ... instead she could only feel affection and sympathy and understanding and know herself utterly unworthy of such loving.

She was both grateful and surprised that he sensed her reluctance to talk of their wedding and did not press her to make the final plans that she had been dreading to face. She was touched by his understanding and his patience. How little the world really knew of Leo—and how badly he was misjudged, she thought with the heat of indignation. He was a kind man, a sensitive and unselfish man, a generous and warm-hearted man ... and she was really very fond of him. Perhaps she should marry him, after all...

Her heart and her mind were so unsettled. She did not know what she wanted, what to do ... all she really knew was that she would never gain what she wanted with all her heart—and she could not help wondering if she would be foolish to spurn all that Leo could offer.

It might not be so difficult to be happy with him ... and what was the alternative? She had agreed to marry him on an impulse—but perhaps she had been guided by shrewd instinct! He would be good to her ... and she asked no more of any man than that he loved her and would keep her safe!

In time, it might even be possible to stop loving Guy who was so hard, so unforgiving, so heartbreakingly indifferent ... and there must be many marriages where love had come after rather than before the ceremony!

It would not be hard to love Leo, surely ... other women had found it easy and so might she have done if Guy had not claimed her heart against her will and even without her realisation...

But she could not find the courage to admit that she had changed her mind nor the courage to declare that she would marry him although she did not love him ... and the afternoon slipped away in lazy conversation and before she realised it, it was time for him to return to town.

She plunged hastily, impulsively: 'Leo ... about Thursday ... Leo, I can't marry you.' He looked at her swiftly; she was not sure if it was anger or pain that touched his eyes. 'Not so soon,' she went on, faltering a little. 'I mean ... my mother may need me and I should like to wait until she is well. You do understand, don't you?'

'Not really,' he said slowly, watching a bird who was busily seeking food among the flowerbeds. 'At least, I understand how you feel, my sweet ... but I can't agree that we need to postpone our plans.' He turned to her, taking her slim hands. 'Darling, I need you,' he said quietly.

She was startled, dismayed. She had been so sure that he would agree to wait ... she had not expected this core of quiet obstinacy in the man who had seemed so willing to please her in every way he could. 'I know, Leo ... but...'

He silenced her with his lips on her own ... a brief, tender but very definite indication that he did not mean to listen to any protests. 'All the arrangements are made. It will be a very quiet wedding and no one will think you an unnatural daughter if you marry the man you love at a time when you may need him by your side.' He smiled at her tenderly. 'You won't be at the other end of the world, my darling, after all ... you can be with your mother very quickly if there is any need for your presence here.' He hesitated a moment and then he added carelessly: 'Carlow is all in favour of it, you know ... he agrees with me that there is no good reason to postpone the wedding.'

Antonia stared at him. 'Guy is in favour? Guy thinks we should carry on with the wedding?' Anger swept through her ... a tidal wave of fury born of pain and dismay and an instinctive rebellion that the two men should decide her future so arbitrarily between them. It did not occur to her to wonder when they had discussed the matter ... or even to doubt that Leo had approached Guy for his opinion. And it certainly did not occur to her that if Guy had been approached and asked for advice he might have allowed his pride to dictate his reply. 'I'm obliged to him,' she said tautly. 'If Guy approves then why should we wait, indeed!' Her voice dripped with caustic irony.

Smiling, he kissed her again ... and the gleam of satisfaction in his eyes escaped her notice for she was almost too angry, too hurt and humiliated, to be aware of him or even to feel the touch of his lips.

Leo had been sure that he need only hint at Carlow's approval to have Antonia quite determined to marry him without delay. It did not matter very much why or when she married him ... as long as she married him. Once she was his wife nothing on earth would be allowed to part them, he thought grimly. He would teach her to love him, he would erase all thought, all desire, all longing for any man but himself from her heart and mind and body ... and in time she would surely be thankful that he had not been sufficiently noble to sacrifice his own and her happiness at the altar of her fancied love for another man...

Antonia was impatient for Leo's departure

... could scarcely wait until his car was receding down the drive and she was free to go to her room and enjoy the fury that was sweeping over her in such waves.

Face down on her bed, too angry for tears, she was quite determined to keep that appointment for the following Thursday ... not because Leo loved her or she thought it might be possible to care for him in time, but simply because Guy had not voiced a single protest and it was utterly hopeless to suppose that she meant or could ever mean anything to him.

She could easily believe that Guy had told Leo that there was no need to cancel the wedding ... he would be thankful to see her married if it took her off his hands and out of his house, she thought angrily, bitterly. Her happiness meant nothing to him—he would not lift a finger to rescue her if he knew with complete certainty that she was plunging into a life of utter misery! He had always disliked her friendship with Leo: he had disapproved of her decision to marry him; he would probably be delighted if all his gloomy forebodings were justified and she regretted the marriage for the rest of her life! He would no doubt feel that she had only come by her just deserts!

She hated him! How dare he push her into this marriage just because he couldn't wait to be free of her? How dare he take it on himself to voice any opinion in the matter at all? It was nothing to do with Guy! If he had not found it necessary to interfere she might have persuaded Leo very easily to postpone the wedding—but with Guy's support behind him and his own eagerness to marry her, it was a combination she could not possibly fight!

Oh, damn Guy! Damn both of them! Damn all men! Guy had caused her a great deal of suffering ... a man who was so incapable of any warm or generous emotion—and she would never forgive him—never! She would hate him until the day she died! If only she could make him realise all that he had spurned, make him sorry that he had failed to love her or to recognise her love for him! How she longed for his heart to ache as hers had ached during these difficult, despairing days ... how she wished it were possible to make him love her and then delight in laughing in his face and dancing gaily off to marry another man!

It would be such a sweet revenge ... and she would not believe that any man could be as indifferent as Guy appeared to be! He had known her for so long and had seemed at times to be carelessly fond of her, to take an interest in her affairs and her well-being.

There was so little time ... but surely it was enough to cause him a few pangs of regret when the day dawned for her marriage to another man? She rose from the bed, her eyes hard and determined ... she had made the mistake of caring too much, she decided. She had failed to win his love in the past because he had sensed the intensity of emotion within her that she had not recognised for herself and he was a man who neither wanted to love or be loved. But now that she no longer loved him at all it might be easier to humble his pride and awaken that cold, unfeeling heart to a new awareness of her value in his life. He could not suspect her of caring for him ... and perhaps he would be more vulnerable to an assault on his emotions!

There must be a way to his heart, she thought fiercely ... and she was determined to find it...

Guy sat at the piano, his hands straying idly over the keys but his attention was caught by Antonia's reflection in a mirror. She was curled in a deep armchair, looking particularly beautiful in a demure black dress, her copper hair banded smoothly about her head. It seemed to him that she had never looked lovelier ... and her beauty, touched with a quiet and serene dignity this evening, caught intolerably at his heart.

He had been surprised when she greeted him with a warm, friendly smile and drew him into light and easy conversation over dinner ... but it had been a momentary

164

flicker of surprise. For this was Antonia, he thought drily. She could not bear to be out of favour in anyone's eyes for very long ... it was more surprising that she had not attempted to win her way back into his esteem before now. As always, it did not seem to occur to her that he might choose to reject the offer of the olive-branch ... and he did not really wish to do so although he realised all the dangers in a return to their former easy intimacy. No doubt he had Bryce to thank for her change of heart, he thought ruefully ... she was happy, looking forward to her wedding day, eager and excited—and in a mood to be at peace with the world.

Chin propped on a slender hand, she seemed to be listening to the music but he suspected that her thoughts were far from his playing or his presence. Her eyes were thoughtful, clouded with dreams ... and his heart wrenched with sudden, sharp pain. How foolish he had been to hope that the day would dawn when that soft and tender glow in her eyes would be born of her thoughts of him, her love for him, her dreams of the future they would know together. He had always known that she was capable of warm and generous loving ... but he had never really imagined that another man might bring it to life. He had always felt that Antonia belonged to him—and that deep in her heart she was aware of that inescapable destiny. He had been prepared to wait until she was ready to admit the truth that they had been born to love each other ... and he had viewed her many light-hearted affairs with other men with tolerance and patience and a supreme confidence.

His confidence had been misplaced ... and he had lost her and he knew that there was no other woman in the world who could take her place in his heart and his life. Very soon, she would be another man's wife ... and it was too late to tell her that he loved her and needed her with every fibre of his being...

'Why didn't you go back to town with Bryce?' he asked quietly. 'Eva is very much better, after all—and you must have things to do before ... Thursday. Or have you changed your plans?'

His voice roused Antonia from her reverie. The music had been soothing, quieting her anger against him, leading her thoughts into treacherous byways ... and she had foolishly allowed herself to dream of the quiet content and security she might have known if Guy had only loved her as she wanted and needed to be loved. But his quiet words shattered the dream and reminded her how little she meant to him, how thankful he would be when she was safely married, how grateful he would be to be free of her troublesome presence beneath his roof and in his life.

But she did not mean him to know that he could wound her with a few careless words. She rose and went to the decanters. 'Of course not,' she said lightly. 'We shall be married on Thursday as we planned. You don't object, I gather?'

'I am not in a position to do so,' he said, a little curtly. 'I am merely your trustee. You are of age ... and quite free to make your own mistakes.'

She carried her drink over to the piano and stood looking down at him, smiling. 'Dear Guy,' she said with light irony. 'So generous...'

There was an expression in those lovely, luminous eyes that he could not analyse. The colour of her eyes could change from grey to green with her moods and he had learned to distrust her when they were green ... as they were at the moment. Green for danger, he thought wryly.

She stood very close to him and there was a warmth in her eyes that he steeled himself to resist. 'When do you mean to go to town?' he asked carelessly. 'You must be very bored with only Eva and myself for company.'

'But you forget Arthur!' she exclaimed, laughing. 'He is a constant source of entertainment, you know—how can you suppose me to be bored?' She met his frowning glance and added quickly: 'Now, don't shoot me down, Guy! I'm not being malicious. You must admit that one seldom has the opportunity to observe the old-fashioned methods of courtship—and I find them rather touching. It might be an excellent thing if some of them were revived by our generation!'

He raised an eyebrow. 'Bryce's courtship seems to have been eminently successful even if it lacked the old-fashioned touch,' he said drily.

Pain flickered briefly in her eyes. Then she returned airily: 'Leo has a great deal of charm—and that is never out of fashion, is it?'

'You must forgive me but I am not at all impressed by that famous charm,' he said brusquely.

She smiled at him with faint mischief. 'Well, you're a man ... you wouldn't appreciate it as a woman does. It's difficult to describe but Leo makes a woman feel ... well, that she's the only one who matters, I suppose.'

'Many men possess that particular talent—but Bryce is certainly more practised than most,' he told her sardonically.

Faint colour stole into her cheeks and her eyes flashed with brief annoyonce at the jibe but she rallied swiftly. 'If you were a woman I should describe that remark as distinctly catty,' she said flippantly. 'And if you were any other man I should suppose you to be jealous of Leo's good fortune!'

'*Any* other man?' he queried mockingly. 'Good fortune? You rate yourself very highly, Antonia.'

She smiled involuntarily, swift to share his humorous reaction to her unthinking words ... but she was faintly regretful that she was still not free of the vanity he had always deplored. 'I wish *you* did not rate me so low,' she said impulsively.

He rose to his feet, smiling ... but a betraying pulse throbbed in his cheek and his smile was taut in the effort to control the tide of emotion that her words had invoked. 'When did you begin to care for my opinion ... good or bad?' he challenged lightly.

'I have always wanted you to think well of me,' she returned quietly.

He touched her cheek with careless fingers, a brief and affectionate gesture. 'And I always have, my dear,' he said steadily. 'You are very dear to me for all your faults, you know.' He smiled down at her. 'And your happiness is very important to me ... so be happy, Antonia.' He turned away and went quietly from the room ... and she looked after him in bewilderment, her fingers instinctively flying to the place where his hand had rested so fleetingly and the heart that had stilled at his touch began to beat once more, heavily, painfully.

Her thoughts and feelings were in utter confusion. The pendulum of her emotions had swung suddenly once more so that she could only think of how much she loved him and how much she needed him to love her! Did he care at all? Surely there had been something in his eyes that she had not seen before—a warmth and a tenderness, something more than ordinary affection. He had seemed so tense, so still—and for a brief moment she had believed that he meant to draw her close, to enfold her in his arms—and then he had left her abruptly, too abruptly, as though he did not dare to stay. Her heart soared with new hope...

He was such a reserved man, always seeking to conceal his emotions. He was so proud—a man who would not admit to hurt or unhappiness or that he wanted a woman who did not seem to want him. He did not know that she loved him, after all. He seemed so self-sufficient—but could it be said of anyone that they did not need the love, the tenderness, the interest and the compassion that others could provide? No man is an island ... Guy must want to be loved, must need to be needed just as much as any other man—and she loved him, she needed him! All she asked of life was that Guy should love and need her in return...

CHAPTER FOURTEEN

Eva wondered if Antonia was really so blind as she seemed to the love that Guy could not help but betray. And she wondered if Guy realised that he exposed his love with every glance, every word ... and she was impatient with him for having left matters so late.

But Antonia was not yet married to Leo Bryce, she thought with a leaping of the hope she had carried in her heart for so long. And Eva could not believe that her daughter was truly in love or looking forward to marriage with any of the delight and eagerness that one expected in a bride. Heaven knew why she had agreed to marry the man ... but perhaps it was not too late for her to regret her promise and to realise that real happiness lay with the man who had loved her so long and so silently...

'Is anything wrong, my dear?' The Commander took her hand as he spoke and leaned towards her anxiously.

She raised his hand affectionately to her cheek, smiled at him with loving warmth. 'No, Arthur,' she said gently, reassuringly. 'Not a thing.'

'You sighed,' he said quietly.

She nodded. 'I was merely wishing that everyone could be as happy as we are,' she told him lightly.

'Your young people, eh?' he said shrewdly. 'Silly young idiots ... stubborn as mules! Eating out their hearts for each other—and too proud to admit it!'

She looked at him swiftly, hopefully. 'Do you think so, Arthur? Do you really think so?' she asked eagerly.

He looked surprised. 'I may be an old bachelor but I've lived long enough to recognise the signs,' he said confidently. 'Too careful with each other, you know ... watching their words, scarcely daring to look at each other, avoiding the accidental touch, keeping it light. They're in love ... you may take my word for it!'

'But Antonia means to marry that dreadful actor,' she wailed. 'How can she care for Guy?'

He shook his head. 'Women are strange creatures ... begging your pardon, my dear. I doubt if Antonia ever meant to marry Bryce ... but I fancy she will if Guy doesn't take steps to prevent it!'

'He's so proud,' she said unhappily. 'It will be a tragedy if he allows her to marry Leo Bryce if it is true that a word from him can stop her. He loves her very much, you know. But Antonia ... oh, I wonder if you can be right, Arthur.' She sighed. 'I don't seem to know anything at all about my own daughter!'

172

She would have been surprised to learn that at that moment her daughter was thinking of her and the Commander with a great deal of envy. They were so close, so dear to each other, so confident in the future ... and she longed with all her heart for the happiness and security that her mother would surely find with the Commander and that only Guy could give her if he chose to do so.

She loved Guy ... she needed him so much. But she still did not know how he felt towards her. Time was running out ... in two days she was supposed to be marrying Leo and she had still not told him or anyone else that she had changed her mind. She knew that Leo must be told and she had made up her mind to see him that very day. She was not looking forward to the meeting, to coping with his disappointment and resisting his persuasions—but there was no alternative. She had deceived him—and now she must be completely honest with him and admit that she had never cared for him, never truly wished to marry him. Perhaps he would suspect her of loving another man but he could not guess that it was Guy who possessed her heart so completely—and she could not explain that she was staking everything on the faint hope that Guy cared for her when that hope was only based on instinct.

If only she could be sure that he loved her ... but there had been no hint of his feelings, no encouragement for her hope, no comfort for her desperate heart. She had given him opportunities, she thought ruefully ... without exactly throwing herself at his head, she had done all she could to break through his quiet reserve, to pierce that seemingly impenetrable barrier of his pride while preserving her own as best she could—and very likely he believed that she was merely indulging in her previous pastime of flirtation.

She sighed ... and gave herself one last glance in the mirror. Then she picked up bag, gloves and car keys and went from the room to keep her appointment with Leo, wondering why life was so complicated for some people and seemingly so straightforward for others...

She avoided the terrace where her mother sat with the man she was soon to marry. She did not want to be questioned about her trip to town ... nor did she wish to explain that when she returned she would be free of her engagement to Leo. In her anxiety to slip away unseen by her mother, she was not prepared for an encounter with Guy and she spun on her heel, startled, when he quietly spoke her name from the doorway of his study.

He looked her over gravely. She looked

very lovely and very elegant in a white linen suit and a wide-brimmed white hat that framed her face. 'You look very bridal,' he said stiffly. 'I thought the wedding was to take place on Thursday.'

'It is ... I mean, it isn't ... it was,' she floundered, dismayed by the coldness of his gaze, his grim expression—and taken aback by his description of her appearance. She often wore white which suited her colouring so well and it had not occurred to her that anyone might suppose she was dressed for a wedding.

'Bluffing the press?' he asked quietly. 'Quite understandable, in the circumstances.'

'No ... oh, no,' she said quickly. 'I'm meeting Leo for lunch, that's all.'

He smiled sceptically. 'Very well, my dear.'

'Oh, don't be silly, Guy,' she said impatiently. 'Why should I wish to deceive you—or Eva?'

'Why indeed?' he countered. 'But I mustn't delay you—you'll be late for your ... lunch.'

She hesitated, wanting to tell him that she did not mean to marry Leo after all and yet too keyed up for her appointment with Leo to trust her emotions if he should demand an explanation. She held out her hand to him impulsively. 'Guy, I can't explain now ...

may I talk to you later?'

He nodded, ignoring that outstretched hand. 'I shall be here, my dear. But you don't need to explain anything to me, you know ... your life is your own.'

She turned away, hurt by the cool indifference of the words. She went out to her car with pain tearing through her that there had been nothing in his voice or expression that she could interpret as regret or sorrow even though he had wrongly concluded that she was hastening to her wedding...

Guy looked after her, his hands clenching fiercely, the agony of loss and despair wrenching at his heart and mind ... and then he returned to his study and closed the door firmly and tried not to think of her return as a married woman...

It was late afternoon when Antonia drove up to the house. Guy looked up at the sound of the car and moved slowly to the window. His lip curled with bitter scorn for Bryce as he saw that she was alone ... and he wondered again that she had chosen to marry a man who allowed her to take second place to his work in the theatre. What kind of a marriage would it be if a man could desert his bride even on their wedding-day and suffer her to return alone to break the news to her family and friends?

He watched her walk towards the house

... and his heart twisted with compassion as he realised her pallor, the weariness that was etched about her mouth, the look of strain in her lovely eyes. He stepped out to the terrace and went to meet her.

Antonia smiled wanly. She was tired and depressed after that difficult and lengthy meeting with Leo for it had not been easy to convince him that she was not suffering from pre-wedding jitters, that she really did not mean to marry him, that she was not likely to be persuaded into loving him eventually if she went through with the wedding. She had hurt him ... and she hated herself for it ... but compassion and affection were no satisfactory substitute for love.

'Hallo, Guy,' she said carelessly, determined to conceal the pain that she felt as she caught sight of him.

'Where's Bryce?' he said grimly.

'Leo? At the theatre, I imagine,' she returned lightly. 'Why?'

'It crossed my mind that he might be with you,' he said drily. 'I suppose I should have known better.'

'You shouldn't leap to conclusions, Guy,' she said wearily, belatedly recalling his suspicion earlier in the day. 'Is Eva in her room?'

'Yes ... she's resting.'

'I'll slip in to see her for a few minutes. I'm going back to town but perhaps you'll give

me some tea before I go. I won't be long.'
She turned towards the house.

'Be careful how you break the news,' he
said abruptly.

She nodded. 'I will,' she called back.

Guy watched her walk into the house. He
supposed it was very natural that she should
wish to talk to her mother before confirming
his suspicion that she had married Bryce. He
must steel himself to wish her happy in all
sincerity however convinced he might be that
she had made a mistake...

Eva could not conceal her relief but she
betrayed very little curiosity and merely
wanted to know if Guy had been told of the
broken engagement.

'Not yet,' Antonia admitted.

'Then you must tell him immediately,'
Eva said firmly. 'I wonder if you realise how
much he has hated your engagement?'

'I knew he disliked it ... as you did,' she
returned quietly. She rose to her feet. 'Yes, I
must tell him ... he is waiting for me now.'
She stooped to kiss her mother's cheek. 'I'm
going back to town ... I shall look for a flat
now that you are getting married. I can't stay
here, you know—and newly-weds don't want
a grown girl about the place,' she added
lightly.

Eva studied her anxiously. 'You are not
very happy, darling,' she said gently.

Antonia shrugged. 'You mustn't worry

about me,' she said tautly. 'I always fall on my feet ... and I'm not unhappy about Leo. I never loved him, you know.'

'Thank heavens you knew it in time,' Eva said with unusual asperity.

'I always knew it,' Antonia told her quietly.

'Then why did you promise to marry him?'

She hesitated with her hand on the door. 'Because he loved me, I suppose. He was kind and affectionate and thoughtful ... and he didn't quarrel with me.' She smiled. 'I found it very boring,' she said lightly ... and went from the room.

She entered the sitting-room to find a tray of tea waiting for her ... but no sign of Guy. She was slightly disconcerted and she felt a pang of disappointment and pain that he obviously did not wish to talk to her. She poured tea for herself and took a cigarette from the box on the table, wondering why she had driven back to Mersleigh End after leaving Leo. A telephone call would have served her purpose. It had really been very foolish to suppose that Guy would immediately notice the absence of any rings on her left hand and catch her swiftly into his arms on a surge of delight and relief and loving thankfulness, she told herself drily.

She covered her eyes with her hand, forcing back the tears that threatened, struggling with the desperate loneliness that consumed her and the fear that she would never know the happiness and security that she knew could only be found in Guy's love and tender protection.

Guy moved swiftly towards her, concerned ... and she raised her head at his approach, clinging to the last shreds of her composure. He looked down at her ... and then he placed his hand gently on her shoulder. 'What is it, my dear?' he asked quietly.

She shook her head, forcing a smile to stiff lips. 'It's been a tiring day,' she said. 'I'm all right Guy.' She glanced at her watch.

'You must be anxious to get back,' he said tautly.

She shrugged. 'I don't want to leave it too late, naturally.' She met his eyes steadily. 'I shall come down for Eva's wedding, of course ... but you won't see very much of me in the future, Guy.' She hesitated and went on: 'You've always been very good to me—and I am grateful, you know. It hasn't been easy for you and I've given you some rough times ... but I do appreciate all that you've tried to do for me.'

He raised an eyebrow. 'Your farewell speech, Antonia ... carefully rehearsed?' he asked mockingly, shaken by the sincerity of her words and by the warmth of her lovely eyes but determined that she should not suspect the turmoil of his feelings. 'I know what it would cost you to admit that you might occasionally have been wrong or misguided in your actions ... so I'll spare you any further sackcloth and ashes.'

She caught her underlip between her teeth to still its betraying tremor as the sneering words struck at her heart. 'You can be very cruel,' she said quietly, painfully.

She looked so genuinely distressed that Guy immediately held out his hand to her. 'My dear ... I didn't mean to hurt you,' he said repentantly. 'I do know what you are trying to say ... and I assure you that there isn't the least need. Your father was my friend—a very dear friend—and I've been glad to do something for him in return for all that he did for me.'

'You have always done it for his sake ... not for mine ... not because I meant anything to you,' she said bitterly.

Guy was astonished—not so much by the words but by the realisation that tears brimmed on her lashes. Almost he caught her into his arms and kissed away the tears and told her roughly that she meant the world to him and always had ... just in time he caught at his self-control and said quietly: 'Antonia, I'm very fond of you ... I've known you a long time. You mustn't suppose that I've resented the responsibility ... I've merely regretted at times that we couldn't agree on the handling of it.'

She sighed. 'We haven't dealt very well

together, have we?'

He smiled ruefully. 'We are too alike—you and I, Antonia. Both proud, both stubborn and both firmly convinced that our individual way must be the right and only one.'

'Oh, yes!' she said impatiently. 'But we might have been friends, Guy!'

He was silent, looking down at her for a long, tense moment. Then he said gently: 'I have always been your friend, Antonia—or you might have gone to the devil a long time ago.'

'Perhaps I did not mean ... friends, exactly,' she said, so low that he scarcely caught the words. 'I wanted you to love me ...'

His heart checked for a breathless moment. Then he told himself that it was second nature to Antonia to cast out lures ... and obviously she would always do so although she had married the man she loved. 'What a child you are,' he said and his voice was tenderly indulgent. 'Everyone must love you—or hate you. You cannot accept that there might be other degrees of feeling ...'

'Such as indifference?' she broke in, her voice tremulous with the desperation of her need to be loved by this man, to know that he loved her, to know herself safe and secure for all time in the quiet harbour of his love. 'And contempt? Must I accept those things without protest, without pain?'

His eyes narrowed abruptly. 'You cannot suppose that I think of you with either indifference or contempt?' he demanded harshly.

She rose to her feet and bitterness touched the faint smile that curved her lips. 'As you couldn't wait to have me off your hands I must assume that you think of me with very little affection or interest.'

He turned abruptly and his hands were suddenly hard on her shoulders, bruising in their fierce grip. 'What makes you think I was anxious to see you married to Bryce?' he asked roughly. 'You know very well that I've longed to put an end to the damnable business!'

Her quick temper caught fire and she flared at him swiftly: 'How can you? You've been pushing me into it from the very beginning!'

He stared at her incredulously. 'Pushing you into it? Because I disliked the man and didn't hesitate to say so? Good God, Antonia—are you so spoiled, so wilful, so stupid that the least opposition can drive you into a man's arms?' He gave her a little shake of exasperation.

She wrenched away from his bruising hands. 'Not opposition ... but approval!' she retorted coldly. 'You gave me your blessing ... what did you expect me to do but leap at his proposal once you'd assured me that I might marry the devil for all you cared!'

He smiled wryly. 'The devil might have been a better choice, my dear. Bryce will make you miserable in a month ... but I'm told that the devil looks after his own!'

A little, involuntary gasp of laughter broke from her lips. Their eyes met in mutual amusement—and then she raised her hand to his cheek in a caress. He stiffened at her touch ... and then he caught her fiercely into his arms and kissed her with a savagery born of pain and jealousy and desperate need.

He released her abruptly ... and she looked up at him in wonderment. 'You do care,' she said softly.

He turned away. 'Your husband is waiting for you,' he said curtly, brutally.

She studied his taut, proud back ... and loved him for his integrity and his pride and his incredible blindness. 'I'm not wearing any rings, Guy ... certainly not a wedding ring,' she told him quietly. She moved to stand before him, offering him her hands. 'I told you not to leap to conclusions.'

'Bryce ...?' he demanded fiercely, searching her lovely face for confirmation of the words he could scarcely believe.

'How could I marry anyone but you?' she asked lightly. 'I've loved you since I was seventeen ...'

He caught her hands and held them in a

184

fierce grip. 'You have to mean what you are saying, Antonia,' he said tensely.

'I love you, Guy,' she said steadily ... and raised her face for his kiss.

He drew her into his arms and held her very close and his lips were very gentle, very tender, very sweet ... and Antonia sighed with content and thankfulness as she stood in his arms and knew herself loved and cherished and secure for the rest of her life. Her heart was home in its quiet harbour after its stormy voyage on the sea of life and love...